She slowly ... and loo...

He looked back, and wh... he saw was a beautiful woman whose hair tumbled around a flushed face, and whose honey-brown eyes had a degree of warmth that symbolized a level of passion he rarely saw.

Enthralled, he held her gaze while his aroused body thickened with each breath he took, wanting more than anything to get naked and sink into the deep, luscious depths of her. He also had to deal with his tongue, the one that'd just spent an ample amount of time kissing her, renewing itself with her taste while imagining another taste he wanted to become familiar with. Her intimate taste. The thought of it made his sex surge and he knew she felt it when it did.

"You're trying to seduce me," she whispered as fragments of passion exploded bit by bit, inch by inch in his stomach from the sound of her voice. He was getting turned on even more seeing her lips move.

There was only one response he could give her, one of complete honesty. "Yes, I am trying to seduce you." And then, helpless to do or say anything else at that moment, he lowered his head to kiss her again.

Books by Brenda Jackson

BRENDA JACKSON

is a die "heart" romantic who married her childhood sweetheart and still proudly wears the "going steady" ring he gave her when she was fifteen. Because she's always believed in the power of love, Brenda's stories always have happy endings. In her real-life love story, Brenda and her husband of thirty-eight years live in Jacksonville, Florida, and have two sons.

A *New York Times* and *USA TODAY* bestselling author of more than sixty romance titles, Brenda is retired from a major insurance company and now divides her time between family, writing and traveling with her husband, Gerald. You may write to Brenda at P.O. Box 28267, Jacksonville, Florida 32226, e-mail her at WriterBJackson@aol.com or visit her Web site at www.brendajackson.net.

NEW YORK TIMES BESTSELLING AUTHOR

BRENDA JACKSON

INTIMATE SEDUCTION

KIMANI™ ROMANCE

To the love of my life, Gerald Jackson, Sr.
To everyone who enjoys reading about the Steeles.
This one is for you.

KIMANI PRESS™

ISBN-13: 978-0-373-86120-0

Recycling programs
for this product may
not exist in your area.

INTIMATE SEDUCTION

www.kimanipress.com

Printed in U.S.A.

Dear Reader,

I knew when I introduced the Steele family that writing Donovan's story would be a challenge. After all, he was the ultimate alpha man, who believed that love was not for him and that there was no woman who existed who could capture his heart.

Of course, I knew differently.

As Donovan watched his brothers and cousins marry, he was determined not to be included in that number. He was enjoying living the single life and didn't see himself being tied down to any one woman. One of the reasons I enjoy writing romance stories is to show how a man like Donovan, who thinks he has it all figured out, can fall victim to love of the most intense kind.

I'm a true believer in love at first sight, but it's hard to convert others. So I will continue to write those love stories where when someone least expects it, love can come knocking on their door…or, as in Donovan's case, come sleeping in their bed.

And to answer all the e-mails I've received asking if Donovan's story ends the Steele series, the answer is a resounding *no*. As in all families, there are other family members and I look forward to introducing you to more Steeles in the coming months.

I hope all of you enjoy reading Donovan and Natalie's story.

Happy reading!

Brenda Jackson

Who can find a virtuous woman?
For her price is far above rubies.
—*Proverbs* 31:10

Chapter 1

Donovan Steele opened the door to his home and walked inside with a huge smile on his face. Over the weekend in New Hampshire, his best friend from childhood, Bronson Scott, one of the most popular drivers for the NASCAR Sprint Cup Series, had placed in the top five.

Donovan was proud of Bronson's success because Donovan, of all people, knew how hard his friend had worked to achieve it. Bronson was not only a skilled driver but was also a racer for the team he owned, Scott Motorsports. Donovan's chest also swelled with pride at the fact that his family-owned business, the Steele Corporation, was a major sponsor of Scott Motorsports. That provided plenty of advertising for SC and offered Bronson the financial support he needed to pursue his lifelong dream.

Another reason for Donovan's smile was that at the race he'd been among friends and had managed to unwind and not think about how busy the coming months would be for him back at the office. A new product under development at SC, the first in several years, had everyone excited; especially Donovan since he headed the Product Administration Division. But Gleeve-Ware, as it was called, had to be completed in time for the annual Product Trade Show being held in Toronto this November.

Instead of returning to Charlotte yesterday like he'd planned, he and a good friend from college, Uriel Lassiter, as well as two of his cousins from Phoenix—Galen and Tyson Steele—decided to stay an additional day to celebrate with Bronson and Myles Joseph, another good friend and a Scott Motorsports driver.

And then there had been Joanne Summerville, a racetrack groupie who'd come on to him after finding out about his close relationship to Bronson and the other drivers. Even now he could still picture her standing under the July sun in those skintight jeans and that sky-blue T-shirt that had stretched snugly across a pair of well-endowed breasts.

Joanne had been a looker, all right, and he regretted not taking her up on what she'd been offering. He hadn't the time to squeeze in a short fling, no matter how tempting, and he could still see the sexy pout on her lips and the disappointment in her eyes when he'd turned her down. His only saving grace was that he figured he'd run into her again at a future race.

Donovan dropped his travel bag on the floor by the sofa instead of taking it upstairs to his bedroom. Due to an early flight out this morning, he'd missed breakfast and was hungry. He walked toward the kitchen, deciding that in desperate times even a peanut-butter-and-jelly sandwich sounded pretty good.

The moment Donovan walked into his kitchen he could tell his housekeeper had been there. Everything gleamed, from the stainless-steel appliances to the ceramic-tile floor. He appreciated the way she kept his house clean. He was a stickler when it came to neatness, but he also liked having a good time and had no desire to spend his weekends doing chores. He was too busy spending his time doing women.

It came as no surprise to those who knew him that he enjoyed and appreciated female company. There was no crime in that and at thirty-three, he enjoyed being single. He spent his time doing things he liked, which included a lot of traveling for pleasure, and refused to be tied down to a woman who'd have a hissy fit if he left her behind or one who felt entitled to accompany him.

He'd learned the hard way that women tended to get outright possessive. Alyson Greer had been such a creature, and even now he got cold chills remembering how she had resorted to stalking him. From that point on, he'd made a conscious effort to make sure any woman he became involved with knew the score.

There were simply too many beautiful ladies out there to get tied down to just one.

His three older brothers were wearing wedding bands and that was all well and good—for them. He was happy they had found wonderful women to fall in love with and marry. But he was not the marrying kind. He wasn't even the serious relationship kind. Short-term affairs suited him just fine.

Besides women, his favorite pastime was auto racing. Not that he would ever get behind the wheel of a race car but he totally enjoyed being a spectator. He couldn't describe the rush of adrenaline that flowed through his body while watching a race. Of course, sharing an orgasm with a woman was still number one in his book, but being at a race was a close second.

He reached to open his pantry when he noticed a pair of women's sandals on the floor by the sliding glass door to his screened patio. Where had they come from and whom did they belong to?

Had the cleaning lady left her shoes? Was she still there?

He picked up the sandals to study their design. Sleek and snazzy. He'd only seen his housekeeper once or twice, and although she wasn't a bad-looking older woman, he couldn't imagine her wearing a pair of stylish and trendy shoes. But then he might be wrong. He couldn't judge every fifty-something-year-old woman by his mother and his aunt's taste in fashion.

He cocked his right brow, his curiosity piqued, and for the moment his hunger was placed on the back burner. He went back into his living room and then the dining room and glanced around, noticing that the rooms were neat as a pin, tidy as could be and well-dusted. That was enough evidence to indicate his housekeeper had been here.

On the main level, he also had a guest bedroom and a spacious bath, with the master suite and his office and another bathroom upstairs. If and when he felt inclined to invite a woman to stay for the night, the downstairs guest room was where they would sleep. He considered it his entertainment room. At one time he'd installed mirrors in the ceiling over the bed until his nephew Marcus—who would come spend the night on occasion—got old enough to question why they were there.

The master bedroom was off-limits. He considered it his personal domain. No woman could lay claim to ever sleeping in what he considered his *real* bed. A number of them had tried, considered it a challenge, their ultimate goal. But so far none had ever made it up those stairs.

After checking the other rooms, he made his way upstairs. It didn't take him long to check the bathroom and his office before heading down the hall that led to his master suite. His bedroom door was closed, which wasn't unusual, but what *was* unusual were the sensations he began feeling in the pit of his stomach, similar to the ones he felt when he was standing on the side-lines waiting for the race to begin.

He opened the door, and his eyes quickly circulated the room, stopping first on the vacuum cleaner that was still plugged into the wall and then on the feather duster that was sitting on his dresser.

He stepped into the room and held his breath when he saw a woman asleep in his bed.

What the hell?

Quickly, he crossed the floor to his bed and stared

down at the sleeping woman. She was definitely not his regular cleaning lady. This woman looked to be in her early twenties and was absolutely, undeniably beautiful.

She was lying on her side but her face was angled in a way that showed an ample portion of it. What he saw flooded his gut with something he'd never felt before, a sensual attraction so hard, gripping and intense that he had to struggle to get air past his lungs.

Her skin, a beautiful chocolate-brown, looked soft, satiny and smooth. Her long eyelashes fanned her eyes, and in sleep she looked totally at peace. Her hair, a dark brown shade, flowed to her shoulders with bouncy-looking curls at the end. He had encountered beautiful women countless times but never before did one have such a gripping effect on his libido. And that very thought downright unnerved him.

Pulling in a deep breath, he inhaled, then took his time releasing it after deciding it was time to wake her. Although his first instinct was to remove his clothes and get into the bed with her. Instead of feeling his privacy violated by the woman in his bed, he was feeling something else altogether. Lust. Bone-chilling, gut-wrenching lust to a degree he'd never experienced before.

He tried tamping down the sensations by thinking that he definitely had a number of questions for her…but first he had to get her out of his bed. With that thought in mind, he reached out and gently touched her shoulder, trying to ignore the way his fingers trembled at the contact. He then watched as she slowly stretched her body before cuddling into another position without opening her eyes.

Tempted to see the rest of her, he slowly lifted the

covers… His sex immediately got hard, pressed tight against the fly of his jeans as his gaze lit on her lush, shapely body. His eyes raked over her khaki shorts and cotton top, taking in her long, toned legs, small waist, curvy thighs and flat tummy. And then there was her scent. It assailed his senses the moment he lifted the covers, a totally feminine aroma that clutched him in blatant desire.

Thinking he'd better do something before he totally lost it, he dropped the covers back in place and gently shook her awake. His fingers trembled for a second time when they came in contact with her shoulder.

He stared down at her face as her eyes fluttered open, blinked a few times, widened and then stared back. The color of flowing honey, her eyes were a perfect match for her complexion. The woman was even more beautiful with her eyes wide open looking like a deer caught in the headlights.

He watched as she opened her mouth as if she wanted to say something but then changed her mind. Instead she moistened her top lip with the flick of her tongue before gnawing nervously on the bottom lip. He felt an immediate tightening in his stomach. An aura of sexual magnetism surrounded them, held them within its grip.

When he couldn't handle the sensations any longer, or the torture of imagining all the things he would love doing to her tongue and lips, he spoke up. "I believe you're sleeping in *my* bed, Goldilocks."

Though her mind was working just fine, Natalie Ford was speechless and incapable of movement.

When she'd opened her eyes, the last thing she expected was to drown in the depths of the most gorgeous pair of dark-brown eyes she'd ever seen. And the man's features were so striking and breathtakingly handsome.

The sensations overpowering her midsection weren't any better. Her response to him was instantaneous and so intense that, until he had reminded her, she'd forgotten that she had fallen asleep in his bed. *His bed*. How embarrassing!

The last thing she remembered was thinking she had finally cleaned every room in the house and had saved his bedroom for last. She was about to strip the bed for fresh linen when something about it beckoned her, invited her to lie down between the luxurious covers. That, combined with the little sleep she'd gotten the night before, had her putting her feather duster aside and sliding between the sheets. The moment her head touched the pillow she had breathed in Donovan Steele's masculine scent. With all kinds of crazy fantasies playing around in her head, she had drifted off to sleep. Now she was wide awake and although she'd never met the man towering over her, she was certain he was Donovan Steele.

Her aunt had three clients who insisted that she handle their housekeeping personally—and were willing to pay extra for that request. Harrell Kelly, Jeremy Simpkins and Donovan Steele. Kelly and Simpkins were professional football players for the Carolina Panthers, and Steele was a successful businessman whose family was well-known in Charlotte. According to her aunt, the three men liked things done a particular way and were determined to protect their privacy. They were her aunt's exclusive clients.

Until her aunt's sidelining injury.

Natalie managed a smile hoping he had a sense of humor because she felt the situation needed it. Tossing the covers aside and pulling herself up into a sitting position, she said, "Break's over. I need to finish this room, which means it's time for me to get back to work."

Thankfully, he stepped back as she eased off the bed. However, he crossed his arms over his chest, looked at her intently and asked, "Do you usually take breaks in other people's beds?"

There was that voice again. Deep, throaty, husky. It was crazy, but she felt as though the sound touched her physically, in some of her most intimate places and in very provocative ways. She wished she could ignore both him and his question as she proceeded to strip the bed. Being handsome was one thing, being over-the-top, teeth-chillingly gorgeous was another. There was no way she could forget he was standing there. He was too overwhelmingly male.

Since she was filling in for her aunt who was home recovering from a broken ankle, this man was technically her employer, and she doubted Aunt Earline would appreciate losing him as a customer. She struck a businesslike tone and said, "No, I don't usually take breaks in other people's beds. That was the first. But then I've never seen a bed quite like yours before."

And that was the truth. Although Donovan Steele was probably six-four, with broad shoulders, he wasn't what she considered big. His bed, however, was huge.

There was no doubt in her mind that four people could sleep comfortably in his bed. She could just imagine what a man—a very handsome one at that—did in a bed this size. Whatever he did, she doubted he did it alone.

"Before we get into an in-depth discussion about my bed, don't you think you should at least tell me who you are, since I know you aren't my regular cleaning lady?"

Natalie stopped and glanced over at him. Not to do so would have been outright rude. The moment her gaze locked with his, she felt sensations she couldn't ignore flood her stomach and her heart rate increased. It should be against the law for any man to look so unerringly masculine.

He had chocolate-brown eyes, a chiseled jaw and a sensual mouth on a creamy cocoa complexion. His hair was cut low and neatly trimmed around his head. A pencil-thin mustache on his upper lip gave him a sexy look. He was wearing a pair of jeans and T-shirt with huge letters that said "Forged of Steele." His scent, the same one that had tempted her to cuddle even more between his sheets, surrounded them.

She inhaled deeply. "I'm Natalie Ford," she said without extending her hand. The bundle of sheets she held to her chest made it impossible to do so anyway and she was glad. The thought of touching any part of him left her off balance.

"And I'm Donovan Steele."

She nodded. "I figured as much. My aunt, Earline Darwin, is your regular cleaning lady. She broke her ankle last week, and I'm filling in while she recuperates. She tried reaching you last week, and when she was unable to do so, she left a message on your answering machine letting you know what happened and that I would be her replacement for the next six weeks."

He kept his gaze fastened to hers as he said, "I left town early Friday morning, and I'm just returning today, so I didn't get any of my messages." He paused for a brief second before adding, "That's mighty kind of you to fill in for your aunt. Will she be okay?"

Natalie was surprised he cared enough to inquire. "Yes, her ankle will be fine as long as she remains off of it for a while. Thanks for asking."

He leaned against the dresser. "Now I have something else to ask. Would you like to explain why you were in my bed?"

She met his dark eyes. "Like I told you, I've never seen a bed like yours before and couldn't help wondering if it was as soft and comfortable as it looked. Once I sat down on it and saw that it was, I was tempted to slip between the covers, and I must have dozed off. I apologize for doing so. It was very unprofessional of me, and it won't happen again."

A look she couldn't define quickly flashed across his face, and she had a feeling he wasn't accepting her apology easily. He continued to look at her for a long time with an intensity that made her throat tighten. But then she felt something else with his stare. Direct heat. And it was getting hotter by the second. She tried to recall when, if ever, a man affected her this way.

"I accept your apology, Natalie Ford."

Natalie blinked, realizing he had spoken. "Thank you, and like I said, it won't happen again."

A slow, sexy smile touched the corners of his mouth. "I think that it will. In fact, I'm counting on it."

It took Natalie a few seconds to recover from the impact of his smile to catch his meaning. When she did, she tilted her head, looked at him and fought the power of his sexuality and the way her body was responding to it. She could tell by the look in his eyes, that deep concentrated stare, that he'd honed in on it too. So, okay, there was chemistry between them. She refused to see it as a big deal. The man evidently was a flirt. "I wouldn't if I were you, or you'll be disappointed," she decided to say.

He lifted his shoulder in a nonchalant shrug at the same time that he shoved his hands into the back pockets of his jeans. "I won't be." An assured smile touched his lips.

For a few timeless moments, their gazes held in a clash of wills. Now she understood Aunt Earline's warning about him. According to her aunt, the man was a bachelor who had quite a reputation with the ladies. Apparently when it came to what he perceived as an available woman, Donovan Steele believed in equal opportunity regardless of sex, religion, race, national origin or occupation, since for all he knew she was no more than someone who cleaned houses for a living. Definitely not the kind of woman a man of his wealth and stature would mess around with.

It then occurred to her that, yes, a cleaning woman would be just the type of woman a man like him would probably mess around with. Discreetly. Not someone he would get serious about and take home to meet his upscale family. He'd be surprised to learn that she had a Ph.D. in chemical engineering and was a professor at Princeton University.

"So, when can I take you out?"

Donovan's question intruded into her thoughts. She studied his face and saw the confidence in the dark eyes staring back at her. No doubt because of the women he'd dealt with in the past, he was pretty sure of himself. He probably figured she was an easy lay and with a few sweet words her legs would part like the Red Sea. Boy, was he wrong.

"I won't be going out with you, Mr. Steele."

He smiled. "Feel free to call me Donovan, and is there a reason why?"

There were several reasons she could give him, with his blatant arrogance heading the list. "The reason I won't go out with you is because I work for you, and I've learned that mixing business with pleasure isn't a good idea."

That response, she thought, sounded more politically correct than what she'd actually wanted to say. "And in addition to that, I'm taking a hiatus from dating for a while," she tacked on for size.

He tilted his head at an angle that made his stare even more penetrating. And then he did something she hadn't counted on him doing. He chuckled. But it wasn't just any old chuckle. It had both a seductive as well as a challenging sound to it. It immediately set her on edge and alerted her to the fact that he didn't consider what she'd just said as obstacles.

He verified her assumptions by saying. "Your aunt works for me. You're working for your aunt. It's not the same. And the only possible reason that I can think of as to why such a beautiful woman like you would want to take a break from dating is because you've dated the wrong men. You're now looking into the face of the *right* one."

Natalie wasn't sure he was the right one, but he certainly was a determined one. Deciding not to waste her time arguing with him, she tightened the bundle of linen she held to her chest and slowly backed up. "I'd better put these in the washer. I'll be back later to put fresh sheets on the bed." She quickly moved to the door.

"Natalie?"

Calling her by her first name was a liberty she hadn't given him but was one he was arrogantly taking anyway. She slowly turned around and once again saw him looking at her. "Yes?"

"Considering the attraction between us, I feel I should give you fair warning that I'm a man who goes after what I want and won't stop until I get it."

She lifted her chin and looked at him while trying to ignore the surge of desire that stirred low in her stomach. There was no way she could deny an attraction existed since the chemistry between them was so blatantly obvious. She of all people understood chemistry and just how reactive it could be.

"Thanks for the warning, *Mr. Steele.*" And then she swiftly walked out of the room.

Donovan rubbed a hand down his face, trying to get a grip. What the hell was wrong with him? To say he was attracted to his temporary housekeeper would be an understatement. Even now he could still feel the heat that had ripped through him when her eyes had opened and latched onto his. And he'd been aroused ever since. Totally, irrevocably aroused.

He pushed away from the dresser he'd been leaning against and pulled in a deep breath. He wasn't a man who pounced on a woman so quickly after meeting her, no matter how good she looked. Usually, when it came to pursuing a member of the opposite sex, he was known to be patient, allowing time for nature to take its course since he was fairly certain how things would eventually end. On the rare occasion when he had to shift things in his favor, he would utilize the art of seduction.

He wondered what approach he would have to take in this situation. For some reason being patient with Natalie Ford just didn't work well with him. He was a goner the moment he had checked out her legs. If he thought they were nice-looking lying down, then they were definitely gorgeous standing up. Most men were inclined to favor a woman's breasts or her backside, but Donovan was definitely a leg man.

He had to admit, though, that her breasts and backside were definitely pleasing to the eyes, as well. He'd gotten a good glimpse of the swell of her breasts through her blouse before she clutched his bed linens to her chest as if they were some kind of shield. And when she had skedaddled out of the room, the way the material of her shorts had stretched across her shapely behind had sent intense heat flaring through him. Just thinking about all her make-a-man-hard body parts fueled his lust.

And he knew women well enough to know she was as interested in him as he was in her. Reading a woman had always been easy for him no matter how coy they tried to be. The courtship game was a phenomenon he'd never gotten right and had never really cared if he did or not. He'd discovered that getting it wrong had never hurt his cause since he usually got whatever it was he was after anyway.

There was something about Natalie Ford that he couldn't quite put his finger on. She had an air of decorum and sophistication that didn't quite mesh with the job she was doing. She had tried using the don't-date-the-employer defense on him, but it hadn't worked because like he'd told her, technically she was not his employee. He would admit that at SC he'd personally instituted a rule about fraternizing with the hired help, a course of action he'd been forced to implement after a number of female employees targeted him as the Steele man to get.

He glanced at his watch. From the look of his home, she was about to wrap things up and would probably be leaving in the next half hour. She had said her aunt would be recuperating for six weeks, and he intended to make sure Natalie didn't try doing a switcheroo on him with another housekeeper.

Just that quick his mind was made up. Natalie Ford was someone he intended to seduce.

Chapter 2

Fighting back a nervous shiver, Natalie quickly moved down the stairs in her haste to get to the laundry room. Her senses felt out of control. Overworked. And all because of one man. She was used to sparring with her students, but sparring with Donovan Steele had rattled her brain.

She should not have been tempted to lie down in Donovan Steele's bed, but her aunt had indicated he rarely made an appearance during the day due to his work schedule. Natalie had erroneously assumed she would be long gone before he got home. How was she to know the man had gone away for the weekend and would come home unexpectedly?

He had found her in his bed, and now the man had all kinds of crazy ideas. Did he really expect her to go out with him? And what she'd told him about taking a hiatus from dating had been the truth. She was yet to meet a man who wasn't threatened by all her successful academic achievements. She had graduated from high school at sixteen and had gotten her doctorate at twenty-one. Thanks to the head of the chemistry department, there had been a job waiting for her when she had graduated.

Although she loved her job, this year things had been rather challenging, trying to teach while providing assistance on a special project for NASA. The university had been glad to loan her expertise to the government but hadn't felt the need to reduce her classes.

Her thoughts shifted back to Donovan Steele, and she couldn't help but make a face. Doing so was childish at best, but at least for the moment it made her forget she was a woman who was very much attracted to him. She fought back a groan. Why her of all people? And why him?

And why did she have a weakness for men in jeans? Especially a man who wore a pair like they were tailor-made just for his body. Firm thighs, lean hips, tight abs. And then there had been those muscles beneath his T-shirt. Although she hadn't wanted to, she had checked him out. Donovan Steele was well-equipped in all the right places.

She wasn't particularly pleased she had noticed that. In fact she wasn't at all pleased that he had made her fully aware of him as a man. She had done a good job over the past few years concentrating on other things besides men. Men, more often than not, were a nuisance, and she'd found it better to go through life trying to forget they even existed.

She glanced down at her watch. It was almost noon, and she had one more home to clean that day. Deciding she needed to finish up and leave as soon as she could, Natalie loaded the washer and was about to put in the detergent and fabric softener when she heard the refrigerator open and close. She didn't have to look around to know Donovan Steele had come downstairs and was in the kitchen.

After closing the lid on the washer, she braced herself before turning around. He was there, looking good in his jeans and watching her—checking her out. And not trying to hide the fact that he was doing so.

"Is anything wrong, Mr. Steele?" She fought to keep her voice even although her stomach churned something awful. And to make matters worse, she was finding it hard to breathe.

With his legs crossed at the ankles he was leaning against a kitchen counter, staring at her and looking as relaxed as any man should be. She wished she could feel as comfortable as he seemed to be.

"No, there's nothing wrong," he finally said smoothly as he popped the cap off a beer bottle. "So, where have you been hiding, Natalie Ford?"

She raised a brow. "Excuse me?"

"I asked where you've been hiding. I'm surprised our paths never crossed before."

Natalie couldn't help but inwardly smile at the absurdity of that. Did the man actually think he should know every single female in Charlotte? Evidently he did. "I doubt we run in the same circles, Mr. Steele. Besides, Charlotte isn't a small town."

She thought about telling him where she lived and

exactly what she did for a living and changed her mind after recalling other men's attitudes once she shared it with them. She was immediately labeled a mad scientist or chemistry geek. Better to let him assume she cleaned houses for a living.

"How old are you?"

Instead of responding, she asked, "How old do you think I am?"

His eyes scanned her face, as if to study her features. Her body warmed when his gaze dropped to her chest and began studying the V of her blouse like the size or shape of her breasts beneath the cotton material would tell him anything. Her throat grew tight, and she felt a hot sensation in the lower part of her stomach. And then, of all things, she felt her nipples harden against her blouse.

"So, what do you think?" she asked in an attempt to direct his gaze back to her face. It was slow in coming, and the smile that touched his lips made her wish she hadn't asked the question since she knew he would read it wrong.

"I personally think they're a nice pair."

She frowned, not believing he'd actually said that. "I was referring to my age, Mr. Steele."

"Donovan," he inserted quickly.

Ignoring his comment, she said, "You were supposed to guess my age."

"Oh, yes, that's right." A wry smile touched his lips, but not at all apologetic. He studied her face again, and she could feel herself blush under his intense scrutiny.

"I'd say around twenty-two or twenty-three."

Natalie wondered if he was being truthful or just trying to be nice. Either way she was truly flattered. "I'm twenty-six."

He took another sip of his beer, and the surprise in his eyes was genuine. "You definitely don't look it."

"Thanks, and how old are you?"

"Thirty-three."

And a very handsome and well-built thirty-three at that, she thought. His sensual chemistry mixed with a hefty dose of raw sexuality, and she was being affected by all that virility. Dragging in a deep breath, she said, "I need to finish everything upstairs and get out of your way."

A disarming smile touched his lips. "You aren't in my way."

But he was in hers, and if she didn't remove herself from his presence she would continue to think about indulging in things she shouldn't. Not only was he challenging her mentally, but he was doing physical things to her—things that no man had ever done before, without a touch, caress…or kiss.

At that moment she felt her lips tingle, and she felt butterflies in her stomach. She glanced at her watch. "I need to wrap things up here to be at my next client's home before two," she said.

"No problem. I'll let you get back to work, but first I need to ask you something."

She stepped into the kitchen and slipped her sandals on her feet. He was watching her every move, staring down at her feet. Then his eyes moved up her legs before finally meeting her gaze again. She slowly arched a brow in response. He had already asked her out, and she had turned him down. She wondered what he had to ask her now. "Ask me what?"

He took another sip of his beer. "I'm sure your aunt explained to you that I'm a man who appreciates my privacy, which is why I want personalized service from the cleaning agency. I don't want just anybody cleaning my home."

She lifted a brow. "Are you saying that you have a problem with me being here?"

"No. You've explained why you're here. You've also indicated your aunt won't be able to do any chores for about six weeks."

She looked at him, wondering where he was going with this. She folded her arms across her chest. "Yes, that's what I said."

"In that case I hope you can understand I expect you to be the one—the *only* one—to handle things here. It would greatly upset me to discover some other person has access to my home."

She frowned. "We have a number of good employees who—"

"Won't be coming here," he said firmly. "Your aunt understood when I hired her agency that I had a problem with a lot of strangers having access to my home, which is why she took on the job herself. Now that she's not capable of doing it, either you take care of things or no one at all."

She tried to keep her frown from deepening. He was trying to be difficult. If her aunt didn't consider him such an important client she'd give him an ultimatum—either accept whatever one of the other Special Touch Housekeeping Agency's employees she assigned to clean his condo or end his association with the agency.

Instead she said, "Fine."

"And I want to increase my services to once a week instead of twice a month."

She had to refrain from glaring at him. His request was ridiculous considering cleaning his home had been a piece of cake compared to the condo owned by Jeremy Simpkins.

He kept his eyes on hers, not for a single second looking away. "Will that be a problem?" he asked.

There was only one answer she could give him. "No, there won't be a problem. Do you want to keep your Monday appointments?"

"Only if I'm your sole client for that day." At her raised brow he clarified by saying, "Just in case you accidentally fall asleep again…in my bed."

Her jaw was set firm when she replied, "Like I said, it won't happen again."

He smiled. "But in case it does."

Natalie inwardly sighed. "It won't."

He nodded, lowered his voice and said, "Regardless. I want you to give this place your full attention. And if you can switch from Mondays to another day of the week. I would prefer it."

"I'll see what we can do," she said, trying to keep the frustration out of her voice.

"Thank you."

"Now I'd like to ask you something," Natalie said, fuming inside.

He waited a long moment before asking, "What do you want to ask me?" He took another sip of his beer.

"Do you normally hit on every woman who crosses your path?"

He gave her that seductive smile again. "Every woman? No. But I don't have any qualms about hitting on a woman I'm interested in. Like I told you earlier, I believe in going after what I want so there're some things I don't beat around the bush about."

"Apparently." And without saying anything else, she moved past him to go back upstairs.

Donovan's lips eased into a crooked smile. "Methinks the lady is just about ready to box my ears," he muttered before finishing off the last of his beer and placing the empty bottle on the counter. Boxing his ears wouldn't be so bad if he got to lock lips with her in the process.

While she was talking, his gaze had been fixed on her mouth. Never before had he seen a pair of lips so deliciously tempting. Just the thought of savoring them, licking them crazy, sent instantaneous heat flooding his insides. Being attracted to any woman was precisely the sort of thing he didn't need right now.

The matters of SC, specifically the product under development, were enough to occupy his attention. The Steele Corporation had been working on Gleeve-Ware and had hired a renowned chemist, Juan Hairston, to create the formula for a highly durable and flexible tubing of silicone, rubber and fiberglass. In its final form Gleeve-Ware could revolutionize the manufacturing industry and push the transportation industry into the next century by the production of a durable, long-lasting tire.

The research, which had begun over a year ago and had been deemed top secret, had gotten unwanted attention when a rival manufacturing company had learned about Gleeve-Ware. They had gone so far as to try and obtain the formula. A high degree of security was in place since SC had decided not to take any chances.

He and his three brothers—Chance, Sebastian and Morgan—comprised the managing body of SC. Chance, at thirty-eight, was CEO. Sebastian, whom they fondly called Bas, was thirty-six and held the position of SC's problem solver and troubleshooter. Morgan was thirty-four and headed research and development. His cousin Vanessa worked for the company as head of PR. The board of directors included, in addition to his parents, his aunt and his two cousins, Taylor and Cheyenne.

The Steele family was huge and close-knit. In addition to the Steeles living in Charlotte, there were a number of other Steeles spread out all over the country. They enjoyed getting together every two years for a family reunion.

When Donovan heard the vacuum cleaner start up, he decided to make the peanut-butter-and-jelly sandwich after all. He may have been overtaken by lust but in no way did he plan to starve over it.

He reached out to open the pantry at the exact moment his cell phone rang. Pulling it off his belt, he checked the ID screen and saw it was Kylie, his sister-in-law. He immediately clicked on the phone. "Tell me you're calling to invite me to dinner." Kylie loved to cook.

She chuckled. "You don't need an invitation to dinner, Donovan. You know you're always welcome. That's not the reason I called. I need a favor."

He smiled. "Anything for a slice of your apple pie."

"Um, I wasn't going to bake a pie tonight, but I'm sure that can be arranged."

"Okay, then, what's the favor?"

"My assistant has a doctor's appointment tomorrow, and there's this huge delivery I need to take over to the hotel and arrange for a business meeting on Wednesday morning. Any other time I would close down the shop while I'm gone, but one of my suppliers needs to deliver some more vases in the afternoon. Chance is picking up the baby when he gets off work, so I don't want to bother him about coming here and covering for me, especially with Alden. You and I know my son's a handful. Since you have to pass here on your way to the Racetrack Café, I wondered if you'd be willing to make a pit stop here and hold down the fort for about an hour or so?"

He'd done so before, last year when she'd been in a crisis. "Hey, that's no problem. What time do you need me there?"

Everyone in the family knew he arrived to work at six in the morning and left at three o'clock, unless some sort of emergency came up. He worked hard but liked playing even harder. The Racetrack Café was jointly owned by several drivers on the NASCAR circuit, including Bronson. It was a popular bar and grill in town and one of his favorite places to eat and hang out. It was customary for him to drop by there every day after work before heading home.

"Around three-thirty."

"I'll be there," he said, already tasting her mouth-watering apple pie.

"Thanks, Donovan, you're a jewel."

"Of course I am. And before you hang up I need to place an order of flowers to be delivered tomorrow to my housekeeper. She's recuperating from an ankle injury."

"Sure. What's her name?"

"Earline Darwin. Hold on while I get her address right quick."

"No need. I've delivered several flowers to her already. Evidently she's a well-liked lady. I'll make sure these get out tomorrow," Kylie promised.

"I'd appreciate it, and will see you tomorrow."

He smiled thinking his brothers had struck gold with his sisters-in-law. Kylie was extra special because not only did she cook mostly every day—and he knew he could drop in for a free meal—but she had made his oldest brother an extremely happy man. The family had all but given up on Chance, who had lost his first wife to cancer and had remained single after Cyndi's death for more than seven years. But he and Kylie had gotten together, had married and now—in addition to Chance's son, Marcus, who was away at college and Kylie's daughter, Tiffany, who had graduated from high school a couple months ago and was currently traveling out of the country with her grandparents—they had Alden, their active two-year-old son. Like most kids his age, Alden kept his parents on their toes. Nowadays, there was never a dull moment at Chance and Kylie's house.

Donovan finally noticed the vacuum cleaner was no longer running when he heard the sound of Natalie's footsteps. He glanced over his shoulder. She stood in the middle of the kitchen with her purse slung over her shoulder, ready to go.

"I'll be leaving now, Mr. Steele," she said in a very professional tone.

He turned to her and smiled. "I'm Donovan. Say it."

He saw the frown that lit her eyes. "I think it's best to keep things strictly business between us, Mr. Steele."

If she was trying to grate on his last nerve, he would not let her. Her attitude only made him even more determined to one day hear his first name flow passionately from her lips. "Okay, but business or otherwise you can still call me Donovan."

"I prefer not."

He moved away from the pantry to come and stand directly in front of her. "Then I plan on working hard to change your mind, Natalie. And I will succeed."

Natalie opened her mouth to give him a blistering retort, to tell him he would fall right on that nice-looking tush of his, but paused. If keeping her mouth shut meant retaining him as a customer for her aunt then she would overlook his arrogant attitude. Instead she said, "I'll discuss your request for increased service with my aunt and determine the days that will work for us and for you."

She turned and headed for the door, fully aware he was right on her heels. Before she reached her destination, he said, "I've thought about it, and I prefer Fridays if that day is available."

She paused and then turned around. "I'll check my aunt's schedule, and I'll get back with you later this week." She knew her tone of voice suggested she wasn't looking forward to doing so.

"Fine, and I'll look forward to receiving your call. And here."

She glanced down at the twenty-dollar bill he was holding out to her. "What's that for?"

He chuckled. "It's your tip. I usually leave it on the kitchen table for your aunt, but since you're the one who cleaned up the place today, it's yours."

She backed up, refusing to take it. "That's not necessary. We bill you monthly for your cleaning service."

"I'm aware of that, but I believe in tipping, as well. Take it."

She started to refuse it again but changed her mind. She wouldn't keep it for herself but would pass it on to her aunt. "Thank you," she said, taking the money from his hand.

Their fingers touched, and the main thing she hadn't wanted to happen did. Sensual energy released in her body, rousing her senses. It had been bad enough to deal with the vibes that had been radiating between them. An actual touch was downright dangerous.

She tried ignoring the reaction and hoped he did, as well, since it wouldn't get either of them anywhere. Unfortunately, she could interpret the look in his eyes. Whereas she intended to ignore it, he planned on doing no such thing. Not only was the man arrogant but he was a rebel as well.

She fixed him a chilly look. "Like I said earlier, I'll get back with you later this week."

"I look forward to your call."

She just bet he did. Fighting back the temptation to say something smart, she turned—without saying another word to him—opened the door and left.

* * *

"How was your first day, Nat?"

Natalie smiled as she looked across the room into the questioning eyes of her aunt. When she'd gotten home after taking care of her last client for the day, she'd found Aunt Earline taking a nap. Natalie had taken the time to prepare something for dinner before her aunt had awakened. The doctors had said the medication for pain would make Aunt Earline sleep for long periods of time. And although Natalie regretted her aunt's broken ankle, she of all people knew this forced period of rest was just what her aunt needed. She'd worked too hard all her life.

It had been her aunt who had taken on the responsibility of raising her as a newborn when Natalie's mother, who'd gotten pregnant at eighteen, had taken a break from the fast life she was living out in California just long enough to give birth to her baby and leave it in the care of her only sister and her husband before taking off again. Over the years her mother had returned on occasion when her money got low, and she would threaten to take Natalie away unless they paid up.

Natalie had been in her teens when her uncle died of cancer but had been only ten when she'd seen her mother for the last time. That was the day Lorene Ford's body was shipped back to Charlotte for her funeral. According to what the police had said when they'd called Aunt Earline from Los Angeles, Lorene's boyfriend had stabbed her to death in a fit of jealous rage.

Last year her aunt, deciding she wanted to be her own boss, had given up her nine-to-five job as a secretary for the school system to start Special Touch Housekeeping Agency. Her aunt was working diligently to build a clientele looking for personalized homecare.

"Today was challenging only because I had to get familiar with the layout of each home and figure out the best way to utilize my time." Natalie finally told her aunt. She saw no reason to inform her aunt that she had fallen asleep in Donovan Steele's bed.

"Mr. Steele was out of town for the weekend and didn't get your message." She couldn't help but smile when she added, "Needless to say, I was definitely a surprise to him."

"I'm sure you were. He's very particular about who cleans up his home. He likes protecting his privacy. I understand the woman from his last cleaning service tried coming on to him, and when he didn't return her advances, she threatened to pass on information about him to the newspaper's gossip column."

Natalie lifted a brow, enlightened. No wonder he was such a hardnose about someone else coming in to clean his place. "He wants to move into a weekly slot. Preferably Fridays."

When she set the cup of tea in front of her aunt, she noticed her frowning. "He wants cleaning service every week?" Aunt Earline asked.

"Yes."

"Why? There's not much to do on the days he's paying us for now. He's a rather clean man, not a slob like Simpkins."

Natalie couldn't agree more. Jeremy Simpkins was a slob, and what was sad was the fact he had a live-in fiancée, so to be fair Natalie wasn't sure which of the two deserved the title. The house had been a complete mess. And it seemed that the two had had a fight the night before. Broken dishes had littered the kitchen floor when she'd arrived. From the looks of things, the argument had started during dinner and had been a doozy.

"Well, that's what he wants," she said, sliding into the chair opposite her aunt with her own cup of tea. It had always been a ritual for her aunt to enjoy a cup of herbal tea in the evening after dinner.

"Then we need to see how we can adjust our schedule to accommodate him. He was one of the first clients I took on, and through him, I got a lot of good referrals. Besides, he pays well and is a generous tipper."

Natalie nodded at her aunt's words. "He gave me a twenty-dollar tip, which I put in the emergency fund jar," she said.

"You should have kept it. You earned it," her aunt replied.

Natalie shook her head. "No big deal." A smile then touched her lips. "He thinks I'm a regular employee with your cleaning service."

Her aunt lifted a brow. "And you didn't set him straight and inform him that you were a chemistry professor at Princeton University?"

Natalie shrugged. "I saw no reason to do that. He can think whatever he wants, as long as he pays for his cleaning service each month."

She took a sip of her tea and, deciding to change the subject, said, "Farrah called while you were asleep. She and I are getting together Friday night and going out."

Farrah Langley was her girlfriend from high

school. While growing up they were thick as thieves, and they made a point to get together whenever Natalie returned to town. She was one of the few people Farrah had confided in when she'd suspected her ex-husband was cheating. And when her suspicions proved to be true, Natalie had been the one who'd provided Farrah with long-distance consolation and support during her divorce.

Aunt Earline smiled. "I'm glad to hear it. I feel bad about you leaving your job to come help me take care of my business. I promise to do everything I can to hurry up and get better."

"And I don't want you to worry about it, Aunt Earline. You need me and I'm here. I had a long talk with Eric last week about my coming here, and staying until you're back on your feet makes perfect sense."

Eric was Aunt Earline's son, who was five years older than Natalie and employed with the State Department as a foreign service officer. He was currently living in Australia.

"Besides, I needed a break from the university anyway," Natalie tacked on. "I did agree to be back in time to do that lecture at the start of the fall semester, and my department head was grateful for that."

Her aunt took a sip of tea and then looked at her and asked, "So what do you think of Donovan Steele? Most of the time I've cleaned his place he's at work. However, the few times I've seen him I found him to be quite a charmer."

A charmer? That was the last thing she'd thought of him. And how did they get back on the topic of Donovan Steele anyway? She shrugged. "I guess some

Chapter 3

"And you actually found the woman asleep in your bed?"

The man sitting across from Donovan at a table in the Racetrack Café rarely showed surprise, but he did now. Bronson Scott had to be the most unflappable man Donovan knew, even when he was behind the wheel in a race car going close to two hundred miles an hour. Regardless of his ability to retain his cool, Bronson did have one major flaw that few people detected. He had a stubbornness that he effectively hid behind a billowy cloud of charisma and charm. He was also loyal to a fault to those he trusted and considered friends. Donovan knew he fell in both categories.

"Yes, she was in the bed upstairs," he responded and watched as Bronson's eyes widened.

"What did you do?"

Not what he'd wanted to do, Donovan thought as he sighed deeply. "I woke her up…after checking her out first. I liked what I saw."

Bronson smiled,. "Regardless, you caught her sleeping on the job, and with your stern work ethic I'm surprised you didn't fire her on the spot."

Donovan was surprised, as well. But there had been something about his Goldilocks that had given him pause…as well as a hard-on that still had her name wrapped around it. How could he explain to his best friend that when he had gazed down at Natalie desire as hot as it could get, as deep as it could go, had blazed through him? And he doubted he could explain why he wanted her back in his bed with an intensity he hadn't felt in years, if ever.

"I could have fired her but I didn't," he decided to say after taking a sip of his beer right out of the bottle.

Bronson chuckled. "And that, my friend, says it all."

Donovan raised a brow. "And what exactly is it saying?"

Bronson leaned back in his chair. "The extent of your interest. That finding her in your bed—that particular bed—has given you what you see as a vested interest in her life."

Now it was Donovan's time to chuckle. "Not her life, Bron, just her body."

There. He'd spoken out loud the very thought that had been running through his mind ever since Natalie Ford had walked out of his door. She was a woman, a good-looking woman, a very hot and enticing woman.

A woman he wanted.

He had decided the moment he'd stared down into her open eyes that he wanted her. Sexual chemistry between them had been thick, the air surrounding them charged. Dangerously so. He would go so far and admit he didn't particularly understand that part of the equation, but he would accept it now and dwell on it later. He knew what he wanted and would act on it. In a way, he already had. She would be in his home at least once a week for the next six weeks. A strategic move that he was pretty damn proud of.

"So what do you know about her?"

Donovan didn't say anything for a moment, thinking about Bronson's question. And then he said, "In addition to having a nice-looking body and a beautiful face, she's twenty-six. Her aunt, my regular housekeeper, hurt her ankle and will be laid up for at least six weeks, and she's filling in to help out."

He then fell silent for a moment as he remembered her in his home. The most prominent memory was how she'd folded her arms beneath her breasts and stared at him with defiance in her eyes. But still, there had been something about her that certainly had his insides simmering in heated longing. He rarely gave any woman a lasting consideration, definitely never thought of plotting the sexual downfall of one, but all afternoon he'd been doing that very thing.

"And I know, by her own admission," Donovan spoke up to add, "that she is currently not seeing anyone. In fact she says she's taking a break from dating."

Bronson lifted his brow. "Why?"

"We didn't cover the details, not that it matters since she will start dating me."

"Good luck."

Donovan took another pull from the bottle and then asked, "Good luck?"

"Yes, I've never known you to get so interested in any woman. The next six weeks should be rather interesting."

Donovan held back the urge to laugh out loud. Instead he said in an amused voice, "And I assume you think that *you* can talk?"

It was a known fact between the two of them that Bronson had fallen hard for a woman named Sunnie, the oldest of the St. Claire triplets from Florida and sister to the wife of Myles Joseph. Sunnie, unfortunately, was playing hard to get, but Bronson was determined to get her anyway.

Just like Donovan planned to get Natalie Ford.

The difference was that Bronson, by a decision of his own, which still had Donovan utterly confused, had allowed himself to get snarled without even putting up a fight. That was a predicament Donovan didn't intend to ever find himself in. He enjoyed female companionship like the next guy—hell, probably a lot more than the next guy—but he knew when and where to draw the line. No woman, no matter how gorgeous her legs were, would get the best of him. In his mind she was a body to be had, pleasured and enjoyed.

"I'm thinking about going to Florida this weekend," Bronson said, breaking into his thoughts.

Donovan was unaffected by Bronson's words. His friend was determined to pursue a woman who didn't want to be pursued.

"I propose a toast," Bronson said, picking up his beer bottle. "To women. The ones we want for whatever reason we want them. May we both be successful in achieving our goals."

Their bottles clinked, and then they both took a huge gulp. The main thought on Donovan's mind as he felt the bitter-tasting liquid flow down his throat was that he would indeed be successful with Natalie Ford.

The next morning Donovan arrived at the office and discovered his calendar was full and that there was an important meeting with his brothers in Chance's office at nine.

He enjoyed arriving at work early, usually coming straight from the gym where he gave his body an intense workout for an hour before showering and dressing to arrive at the office by six.

His secretary usually got in around eight, which meant he had a couple hours to handle whatever was at the top of his "must take care of" list without any interruptions. There was a time Sebastian and Morgan would also arrive around six in the morning. But since they got married, they seemed reluctant to leave their wives any sooner than they had to. Since Chance had been a single dad with a school-age child to handle, he'd preferred flexing his hours to suit his needs, which had been understandable. Nowadays he still flexed his schedule due to Alden. Either he took him to the nursery each day or picked him up. Donovan could tell his brother enjoyed stepping back into the role of father to a young child.

Donovan sat down at his desk with a cup of steaming coffee in his hand and rolled his eyes at the mere thought of any woman keeping him in bed beyond what he deemed was necessary. Men had a tendency to get too carried away with the opposite sex. Hell, they got carried away with sex period…or in his case, as he would admit grudgingly, the thought of getting sex.

That made him think of Natalie Ford. Hell, he had thought endlessly about her last night, if the truth be told. And alone in his office with just his thoughts, he might as well tell it. He had dreamed about her and her legs. He had even gone farther than that by thinking about the juncture of those legs and how he'd love to lose himself in that section of her body. A part of him wished she had not changed the linen on his bed. Instead of welcoming the clean, fresh scent when he'd gotten between the sheets, he had longed for her scent, a reminder that she had been in his bed.

But even without her scent as a memory, he had remembered. He had remembered to the point where he'd gone to sleep with a hard-on as a result of thinking about her, recalling what he'd seen when he had lifted that bedspread off her while she slept. She had looked so damn good in her shorts and top that he couldn't help wonder just how she would look naked.

He was so enmeshed in those thoughts that he jumped, almost spilled coffee on his shirt, when there was a knock on his door. He frowned and glanced at the ceramic clock on his desk, a birthday gift from Lena, Morgan's wife. It was a joke in the family that he enjoyed watching time slip by. It was early—a few minutes past six. Who else would be in the office this early other than security?

"Come in," he yelled out.

He was surprised when Sebastian stuck his head in the door, before opening it wide to walk in with a cup of coffee in his hand. Donovan sat up straight in his chair and quickly slipped the piece of paper he'd been doodling on inside his desk. Absently, he'd been jotting down all the ways he'd like to do Natalie. He was a master when it came to lovemaking positions and wanted to try each and every one he could think of on her.

"Why are you here so early?" he asked as his brother shut the door and eased down in the chair across from his desk.

"Jocelyn has a doctor's appointment later today, so I thought I'd come in early and get a few things done before I have to leave."

Donovan nodded. It was hard to believe how things had changed for Bas since getting married. There used to be a time when the Steele Corporation was more than a company to Bas; it had been his lifeline. Bas had been the last Steele brother to come work for SC. Of the four of them, it had been Bas who'd given their parents the most grief while growing up, especially during his teen years. Bas and the old man used to butt heads all the time, mainly because trouble had a way of finding Bas at every turn.

Now Bas was a happily married man with a baby on the way.

"Everything's okay with Jocelyn and the baby?" Donovan asked.

Bas smiled. "Yes, everything is fine. Since she's due next month, the doctors are now seeing her each week."

"And you still don't want to know if you're having a boy or girl?" Donovan asked, then took a sip of his coffee.

"Nope. We'll find out soon enough."

Donovan nodded. That was the same attitude his other brother Morgan and his wife, Lena, had taken. Lena was due to deliver a month or so after Jocelyn.

"All we know is that it's one big baby. No triplets for us," Bas added jokingly. Donovan understood the punch line. Their cousin Cheyenne had given birth to triplets nearly nine months ago. The first multiple birth ever recorded in the Steele family.

His conversation with Bas easily shifted into details about the race that past weekend. Everyone was happy about Bron's win and the positive exposure it had given SC. It was good advertising dollars at work.

"Do you know what our meeting this morning with Chance is about?" Donovan asked, knowing if anyone knew it would be Bas. As company troubleshooter, he kept well informed of anything and everything that happened at SC.

Bas shrugged. "Chance will tell you everything you need to know soon enough."

Donovan rolled his eyes, wondering why he'd even bothered to ask. When it came to sharing SC's business with anyone, Bas always developed a case of locked lips.

"Well, I'd better get to my own office. I have a lot to do," Bas said standing.

Donovan inwardly smiled. It would be just like Bas

to put distance between them for fear of him trying to pump him for more information.

"Okay, then. I'll see you at the meeting," he said when Bas turned to leave. Donovan lifted a brow wondering what suddenly had Bas so nervous.

Natalie sipped her coffee trying to decide when would be the best time to call Donovan Steele. She and her aunt had worked on the schedules, and after shifting a couple of customers from Friday to Thursday—with their consent, of course—they had come up with a workable solution to accommodate Mr. Steele's request.

She was working on the inside today, from the office set up in her aunt's home, doing payroll and ordering supplies, and had been, for the time being, successful in talking her aunt into taking it easy and getting some rest.

Checking the clock on the wall once again, she figured Mr. Steele should be in his office by now and decided to give his business number a try. Taking a deep breath, she picked up the phone, glanced at the business card her aunt had attached to his file, and punched in the numbers. It didn't take long for his secretary to answer.

"The Steele Corporation. Donovan Steele's office. May I help you?"

"Yes, may I speak with Mr. Steele?"

"Who may I say is calling, please?"

"Natalie Ford."

"Please hold on, Ms. Ford."

Natalie pushed away from the desk to glance out the window, trying to get her mind off the fact that in a few moments she would be hearing the sound of Donovan Steele's voice again. Maybe she was suffering from a case of concentrating too much on work and not enough on the opposite sex. Why else would the sight of a good-looking man with a sexy voice have her mind flipping around like a fish out of water?

It wouldn't take much to close her eyes, recall and visualize yesterday's encounter with Donovan Steele. After leaving his place, driving over to her next client's home had been difficult. She'd been overheated. Blatantly hot. If she could have gone somewhere and stripped down to her panties and bra she would have been tempted to do so.

And the sad thing about it was that her body's high temperature had had nothing to do with Charlotte's weather. It had been a hot day in July, true enough, but not a scorcher. She could now attribute her fever yesterday to Mr. Steele.

Mr. Steele.

He had tried several times to get her to call him Donovan, and she had refused to do so—would continue to do so. To call him by his first name sounded too personal, and she didn't want to have that kind of relationship with him. She refused to have any sort of a relationship with him.

Her thoughts snapped back to the present when she heard the phone click in her ear and then… "Hello, this is Donovan."

Immediately, her heart began pounding, and even though she didn't want it to, her body began heating up, similar to the way it had yesterday. The man had such a sexy voice.

"Hello."

At the sound of that voice again, she suddenly realized that she had not responded to his first greeting and quickly said, "Yes, Mr. Steele, this is Natalie Ford from Special Touch Housekeeping Agency."

"Yes, Natalie, what can I do for you?"

His words flowed across her body like a stroke of some explosive fluid to a simmering brushfire. She'd never concentrated on the sound of a masculine voice before, especially not to this degree. And the sound of one had definitely never even come close to giving her a sexual thrill. For her to come this unglued meant she had gone without male company too long. What had it been now? Five years?

"Natalie?"

She sighed and pushed a lock of hair back from her face while trying to ignore the way he said her name. His sensuous tone stroked something within her that so far no man ever had stroked fully before.

Passion.

While growing up she'd known about her mother's wild and reckless ways, and had gone through life determined not to make the same mistakes Lorene Ford had made when it came to men. As a teen, instead of letting the pursuit of boys occupy most of her time, Natalie had found solace in her books.

And when she'd gone off to college, being younger than the other students had been challenging. That's when she had met Karl Gaines. Like her, he had been totally absorbed in his books…or so she had thought. She had found out the hard way that he'd been just as cunning, controlling and manipulating as he'd been brilliant.

And he had been cruel. He had eroded her confidence as a woman and her ability as a mate to keep the man she loved satisfied sexually. He hadn't minced words when he'd talked about her lovemaking abilities, or lack of them.

Even with the disappointment of that brief affair with Karl, Natalie truly believed that somewhere deep inside of her an intense amount of stored-up fire was just waiting to be released. But she was determined to keep it under lock and key, although a part of her yearned to set it free.

"Yes, Mr. Steele," she finally said, determined to keep things on a professional level between them. "I'm calling to let you know that Special Touch will be able to accommodate your request to have one of our employees—"

"One of your employees?" he cut in sharply to ask.

Natalie knew why he'd done so and modified her words. "*I* will be there every Friday, and when my aunt gets back on her feet, she will resume her duties as your personal housekeeper."

There. She hoped he was satisfied. She shifted, uncomfortable in her chair suddenly, feeling as if she'd just placed herself at his beck and call for six weeks. She shrugged off the idea, thinking that she would probably be in his home no more than two to three hours each week.

"That sounds better, Natalie. A whole lot better. Thanks for calling to inform me of the change. It says a lot for your aunt's agency to try and work with her clients this way."

Natalie rolled her eyes. "We aim to please," she said tartly and immediately saw the error in doing so when he replied.

"Aim to please? Um, that's good to know. Goodbye, Natalie."

"Goodbye, Mr. Steele."

Natalie hung up the phone thinking at least she had gotten through the conversation relatively unscathed and not feeling as if she'd been stripped naked. But for some reason she had been left with the impression that she wouldn't be so lucky the next time around.

Donovan leaned back in his chair after ending his call with Natalie. It somewhat amused him that she still refused to call him by his first name: but all that would definitely change after they shared their first kiss. After that, not only would she say his name but she would be purring it.

He closed his eyes to recall some of the finer details of yesterday. He moved past the episode of discovering her in his bed—but only because that segment had consumed his entire mind most of yesterday and the majority of last night. Instead he chose to fast-forward to when he'd come downstairs to find her in his laundry room bending over while loading his sheets into the washer. He was surprised he was still breathing. Never before had a pair of legs seemed so in sync with a lush behind. He had immediately grabbed a beer out of the fridge. It was either use the cold drink to cool off or take the chance of burning to a cinder. He remembered too when he had stood in front of her, right before she'd made a fast exit for the door. He'd had come close to leaning in and kissing her.

"Mr. Steele, your brother phoned to remind you of the meeting in his office at nine."

Upon hearing his secretary's voice, Donovan opened his eyes, and his gaze immediately landed on the clock on his desk. It was ten past nine. "Let Chance know that I'm on my way, Sandra."

He quickly stood, and before reaching the door grabbed his jacket off the rack. It was unlike him to be late to a meeting. How could he let fantasies of a woman who was playing hard to get totally swamp his thoughts?

A profound edginess flowed through him as he made his way down the hall toward the elevator. He refused to let Natalie Ford turn his entire life topsy-turvy. No sooner had he made that vow when he felt heat suffuse his body at the thought of all the wild sex he planned to have with her once he seduced her. Just thinking about those legs that he liked so much being wrapped around him while he made love to her seemed to boost his energy level.

He stepped into the elevator thinking next Friday couldn't get there fast enough.

"So where do you want to go Friday night?"

Natalie resisted the urge to tell Farrah nowhere. Although she much preferred staying in and curling up with a good book, she knew she and Farrah needed to get together. They hadn't seen each other since Christmas, the last time Natalie had returned to Charlotte. Besides, Friday would be exactly a year to the date that Farrah's divorce from Dustin had been final. That wouldn't have been so bad if Dustin had felt any remorse for cheating on his wife. Instead, once Farrah had confronted him with her suspicions about his extramarital affairs, he hadn't tried to deny them, nor had he apologized for breaking his marriage vows. Instead he informed his wife of four years not to waste time forgiving him since he wanted a divorce to marry the other woman—the woman who'd had his child. And he'd done just that—less than a week after his divorce had been final.

"Natalie?"

Natalie blinked and stared down at the speaker-phone on the desk, realizing she hadn't answered Farrah's question. "Doesn't matter. Wherever you want to go is okay with me."

"Um, in that case, Nat, I want to go somewhere there will be a lot of men."

Natalie could only shake her head while thinking that Friday would be one of those nights. Last July she and Farrah had met in New York for the weekend to do some shopping and take in a play. She had let Farrah talk her into going to this nightclub in Harlem, and the two of them, along with several very handsome men, had danced the night away. Her feet actually ached at the memory. She smiled when she remembered the disappointed faces of the men who'd thought they would be getting more from her and Farrah than a few dance moves.

"That's fine. You pick the place," she decided to say, shifting her gaze to the flowers that had just been delivered to her aunt. They were from Donovan Steele. She could tell her aunt had appreciated the man for being thoughtful enough to send them.

"Um, what about the Racetrack Café?"

Farrah reclaimed Natalie's attention with her question. She had heard about the Racetrack Café but had never been there since it had opened up after she left town for college. From what she'd heard, it wasn't your typical sports bar and grill. She understood the food was good and the atmosphere friendly. And usually there were more men there than women because on occasion a well-known race-car driver would drop by.

"The Racetrack Café sounds like a winner to me as long as you don't plan to dance all night."

Farrah's laughter came through the speakerphone. "I promise I won't."

"Glad you could join us, Donovan."

Donovan couldn't help but smile at his oldest brother. Even if Chance hadn't been born the oldest, he would still be the perfect one for the CEO role. He was a born leader, and Donovan would admit grudgingly that Chance was one of the few people who could keep him in line. Most of the time. Bas and Morgan knew it was a lost cause.

"Sorry, I got somewhat detained," he responded entering the room and closing the door behind him. As he took a seat, he glanced at the others already there—Bas, Morgan and Vanessa—who no doubt had been on time. Unlike his two brothers who were staring at him, Vanessa had chosen to pass the time by messing with her BlackBerry.

She'd only been married a year, and if he were to guess by the way her thumbs were working, she was sending her husband, Cameron, a dirty little text message. The way her lips tilted at the corners in a devilish smile all but confirmed he was right; whatever message she'd sent had been hot and sleazy. He of all people knew just how that part of a person's mind worked.

Since she had been too busy texting to notice he'd arrived, he said, "I'm here now, Vanessa, so you can stop texting Cameron those pornographic messages."

She snapped her head up, glared at him and then opened her mouth as if to deny that was exactly what she'd been doing. And then as if she'd thought about it for a quick second, she closed her mouth and the glare slowly vanished from her face. She tilted her head at an angle and lifted her chin. "Doesn't matter. We're married now," she said haughtily.

"Thank God."

That had come from Morgan and understandably so. Cameron was his best friend, and he of all people knew how long it had taken Cameron to win Vanessa over. As far as Donovan was concerned, it was too long. It was his opinion that no woman had been or currently was worth all of that.

"Now that we're all here," Chance said, before anyone else could make a comment. "I'm turning the meeting over to Morgan. Since he heads the research and development department, he will bring us up to date on some information we received this weekend regarding Gleeve-Ware."

Donovan shifted his gaze to Morgan. Not for the first time he wondered how Morgan did it. He was a father-to-be, worked hard for SC and in addition to that, he was a political figure in town. He had won a council at-large seat last year. Where did the man get all his energy?

"I wanted to bring something to your attention," Morgan was saying. "I got a call from Juan on Sunday morning. Someone tried to break into the lab Saturday night. The alarm sounded but nothing was taken. He just wanted to make us aware that someone is interested in what we have going on with Gleeve-Ware and will probably stop at nothing to get the formula."

Donovan nodded. Morgan had gone to college with the chemist, Juan Hairston, they had hired to head the Gleeve-Ware project. "What do you need from us to make sure that doesn't happen?" Donovan asked.

"All the appropriate steps have been taken to protect and maintain the secrecy of the chemical process formula, but still, I'm encouraging everyone to keep your eyes and ears open and report anything suspicious to Bas since he's our troubleshooter working with security," Morgan said.

"And, Vanessa, I suggest you get with Holly Brubeck in HR to make sure we're doing periodic security checks on any employee with access to our trade secrets, and to make sure all employment applicants sign confidentiality agreements. The last thing we want is to hire someone whose goal is to steal the formula for Gleeve-Ware right out from under our noses."

Vanessa nodded. "Is there anything else you want me to do from a PR standpoint?"

"No, but don't be surprised if we suddenly start getting painted with a negative brush," Chance responded to say. "If the culprits can't get the information they want, they might resort to smear ads or negative accusations."

"Like they did a couple years ago when they put out the rumor we were outsourcing," Bas added, reminding everyone.

The meeting lasted for another half hour when other business matters were discussed. Right before Chance closed the meeting, Donovan spoke up. "Just an FYI. I will be working from home on Fridays for the next few weeks."

Bas raised a brow. "Is there a reason why?"

Donovan smiled at everyone who was looking at him. "No reason."

But he knew his brothers knew him well enough to know such a move probably involved a woman.

And they were right.

But they had no idea that he was meticulously planning the intimate seduction of one Natalie Ford.

Chapter 4

"If you need to reach me, Donovan, just give me a call on my cell phone," Kylie Steele threw over her shoulder as she quickly headed for the door. "You probably won't get many customers, and most of them will be phone orders instead of walk-ins. See you later." And then she was gone.

He chuckled as he took the stool behind the counter and watched his sister-in-law pull out of the parking lot. He'd covered for her before and knew what to do. He had an hour or so to kill until she returned so he might as well make the best of it, and with the flat-screen TV on the wall directly behind him, at least he wouldn't get bored.

To kill some time, he took his BlackBerry out of his pocket and scrolled through his text messages. Most of them were from Joanne Summerville, the woman he'd met at the races this past weekend. He hoped she wouldn't start making a nuisance of herself. He could definitely do without that type of woman.

A half hour later he had put his BlackBerry away and his attention was concentrated on the television, namely CNN, thinking it was a damn shame Soledad O'Brien was a married woman. He was about to scoot the stool closer to the television for a closer view of her when the jingle of the bell above the door alerted him that he had a customer. He glanced up and saw an elderly woman with a cane stop in her tracks when she saw him.

"Where's Kylie?" she asked him accusingly.

He lifted a brow. The way the woman had asked implied she thought he had done away with his sister-in-law. "She had to step out," he decided to answer to assure her misplaced fears. "May I help you?"

She frowned at him. "And who are you?"

The woman sure asked a lot of questions. He wondered how long it would take for her to place an order and leave. She was presently standing in the way of him and Soledad. "I'm her brother-in-law," he said, hoping that would allay whatever problems she had with him.

He watched, surprised, as a slow smile replaced her frown. "Oh, you're one of those Steele boys."

He chuckled. He hadn't heard him and his brothers described just that way in a long time. Of the four of them, most people knew Bas mainly because while growing up he'd had a reputation around town for getting in all kinds of trouble. "Yes, ma'am, I'm one of those Steele boys."

"And which one are you?"

"The youngest."

She nodded. "Oh, you're the one who likes the girls."

That was him, all right. He lifted a brow, wondering just who this woman was. One thing was for certain; she had just made a pivotal point about him and he had no problem admitting it. "Yes, ma'am, I'm the one who likes the girls."

"Just like Drew did in his day."

Donovan couldn't help but laugh. Drew Steele was one of his father's cousins, and from what Donovan had heard, thirty years ago Drew had had to leave Charlotte when a bunch of women threatened to do him bodily harm because of his notorious reputation. Drew escaped to Phoenix, eventually married and had a slew of kids.

"Yes, just like Drew," he said, not the least bit ashamed to claim such a thing. What he didn't say was that, unlike Drew, Donovan felt he had his game together and didn't intend to get run out of town by a bunch of women. Times had changed. Most men weren't seeking a woman's undying love and affection—just a chance to share her bed. He made a point to make sure the women he messed around with knew the difference.

"I take it you knew Drew," he said, indicating the obvious.

The frown returned to the elderly woman's face. "Oh, yes, I knew Drew. He would have messed up my daughter's life if we hadn't sent her off to school in Florida with my sister. She was so convinced she was in love with him and that he loved her. Everyone in town knew he didn't love anyone but himself. That was over thirty years ago. She eventually married and got on with her life."

Donovan nodded, happy for her daughter. There was no need to tell her that although Drew had pretty much settled down some of his sons were following in their father's footsteps. "Did you want to place an order?" he decided to ask her.

She slowly began moving toward the counter. "Yes, I got a sick church member, and I want to send her a bunch of those flowers over there," she said, pointing to the refrigerated glass case containing an assortment of flowers prearranged in a ceramic vase. "Any ones will do in the twenty-dollar price range."

"All right. Do you want to take them with you?" he asked, writing out the order form.

"No, I want Kylie to have them delivered for me," she said and then handed him a slip of paper.

He glanced down at it. "Earline Darwin?" he asked. Of course he recognized the name.

"Yes, you know her?" the elderly woman asked.

"Yes, I know her." *But I want to get to know her niece even more.*

"Did you get a lot of orders while I was gone?"

Donovan glanced up when his sister-in-law walked through the door. "Around three phone orders and only one walk-in. A Ms. Hayes stopped by to send a bunch of flowers to Earline Darwin."

"Like I said yesterday, Ms. Darwin is a popular lady. I'll make sure she gets them tomorrow," Kylie said, moving to the register to close it out for the day.

"No need. I'll drop them off on my way home." Donovan figured Natalie would be there taking care of her aunt since she couldn't get around much.

Kylie tilted her head to look up at him with a bemused look on her face. "Why? Did Ms. Hayes say she wanted them delivered today?"

"No, but I thought I could do that and also check on Ms. Darwin."

Kylie crossed her arms over her chest. "Okay, what's going on here, Donovan? You're a nice guy and all but what's the real reason you're dropping by Ms. Darwin's home? And I recognize the address. It's not on your way home, nor is it close to the Racetrack Café. So just what are you up to, Donovan Ridge Steele?"

Donovan tried hiding his smile by looking down at his feet. He'd gotten caught so he might as well come clean. Besides, this was Kylie. Since marrying Chance, she'd had two teenagers in the household to deal with—teens that Donovan had discovered could be as conniving as they came.

He lifted his head to meet Kylie's questioning gaze. "I told you that Ms. Darwin is my housekeeper."

She nodded. "Yes, you did mention that."

"Well, what I probably didn't mention is that her niece is filling in for her for the next six weeks."

He watched as understanding shone on Kylie's face. "She's pretty, I imagine."

"Very."

Kylie frowned. "And knowing you like I do, I guess that means you want to add her to your 'get-her-in-my-bed' list."

He wondered what Kylie would think if she knew

Natalie had already been in his bed; however, he hadn't been in it with her. "Aw, come on, Kylie. You make me sound like the rake of the year. I'm very up-front with any woman I become involved with. I tell her what to expect and what not to expect."

"But that's no guarantee that they won't fall in love with you anyway. I don't want to remind you about Alyson Greer."

Donovan rolled his eyes. "Please don't bring her up. And I did explain to Alyson how things would be, but she refused to take me at my word because she had her own agenda. What you don't want to accept, Kylie, is that there are women just like me out there who don't want a lasting relationship any more than I do. Those are the women I deal with. Plain and simple."

From her expression, he could tell his words hadn't been too convincing so he said. "Trust me, Kylie. It's not that serious."

She lifted a brow. "I don't know about that, Donovan. I'm the mother of a daughter whom I want to be aware of men like you."

His grin didn't waver since he didn't take her words as an insult. "And your daughter has an uncle who would defend her honor to the hilt if he had to. But, again, the women I deal with know the score. If they choose not to believe what I tell them, or if for some reason they get it into their heads that I'm a man who can be caught and tamed, it's their fault and not mine."

He and his sisters-in-law had had this conversation several times before, and his stomach knotted at the awful memories. One night they had cornered him and all but made him promise to be considerate of women's feelings. It had taken him a full hour or so to convince them that he was.

He watched as Kylie sighed in frustration before walking over to open the glass case. "I hope you know what you're doing, Donovan. I have a feeling that one day will be payback for you, and some woman is going to break your heart."

He chuckled. "Trust me, sweetheart, it's not going to happen."

"Aren't those flowers just lovely, Nat?"

Natalie smiled as she placed a bowl of soup in front of her aunt while glancing at the flowers that had been delivered earlier that day from Donovan Steele. "Yes, they are pretty, Aunt Earline. But then all your flowers are simply beautiful."

And she had received quite a few from various church members, neighbors and friends. Natalie had a feeling why her aunt thought the ones from Donovan were so special. Because she hadn't expected them. There certainly hadn't been any flower deliveries from Kelly and Simpkins.

"I need to send him a thank-you card."

Natalie knew it would be a lost cause to tell her aunt there was no hurry in doing that, so she didn't.

"You got two calls today from potential clients. I got their addresses to mail them out a brochure," she said sitting down across from her aunt at the table.

"Thanks."

"And the Baxters called to cancel their service on Thursday. They're going out of town."

For the next hour Natalie brought her aunt up to

speed on everything that had happened that day with the business including the bad news that they'd received a resignation from one of their employees whom they considered dependable.

"I hate that Lola will be leaving us in the fall, but I'm glad she's decided to return to school. She only has a few credits left before she gets her college degree. And at least she gave us a lot of notice for us to find a replacement."

And then it was time for her aunt's afternoon nap. After making sure she had taken her medicine and was comfortably settled in bed, Natalie was just leaving her aunt's bedroom and closing the door behind her when the doorbell sounded. Not wanting the sound to disturb her aunt, she quickly headed toward the front of the house, wondering if one of her aunt's church members had come calling.

She glanced out the peephole in the door, and her chest immediately tightened. Donovan Steele was standing on the porch. What on earth could the man want? Glancing down at her skirt and blouse, and deciding she looked decent enough, she quickly ran her fingers through her hair and then she inhaled deeply before slowly opening the door.

Before she could ask why he was there, he handed her a vase of flowers and said, "I thought I'd help out my sister-in-law by delivering these."

It took all of Donovan's self-control not to pull Natalie into his arms for the kiss he'd been aching for since meeting her yesterday. It was insane. Yet, for one tantalizing minute he wanted more than anything to pull her into his arms to find out if her lips were actually as soft and delicious as they looked.

It would be a provocative move. Bold. Totally out of line. Considering such a thing should give him pause. Unfortunately, what it was giving him was an ache right behind his zipper, which he was trying like hell to fight back.

He was fully aware of her, although he was trying so hard not to be. She looked cute in her skirt and blouse. In truth there was nothing unusual about them. Still, they stirred raw desire within him. But when you had legs that looked like hers and a body that could make a man drool, it was hard not to be fully aware of anything she wore. Even a potato sack if she chose to don it.

"You work with your sister-in-law part-time?"

Her question brought his attention back in focus and away from her legs. "Not really," he said, deciding to lean against the porch column for support. "She had something to do today, so I did her a favor by watching the store for an hour or so. One of your aunt's church members dropped by and ordered these flowers. I couldn't resist delivering them in person."

Her eyes shone bright in the fading sunlight. "And why couldn't you resist delivering them?" she asked.

He could feel her nervous tension and watched as she licked her top lip with her tongue and felt his gut tighten even more. Her luscious scent surrounded him, made him appreciate being a man who was intent on having her. "Because I figured you would be here, and it gave me a chance to see you again," he finally said, watching her reaction to his words with a steady gaze.

She opened her mouth as if not believing what he'd

boldly stated. Then she closed it, paused momentarily and said, "Mr. Steele, I think—"

"Donovan. That's what I want you to call me. What will it take for you to do so, Natalie?"

He observed the narrowing of her eyes, the tightening of her lips. She wasn't too happy with him now. Just as well since if the truth be told, he wasn't too happy with her, either. She was being difficult, playing hard to get. Normally he liked the challenge, but in this case, although he'd only met her yesterday, she had made an impact, and his patience was wearing thin.

He decided to press on while he had her at a loss for words. "Are you going to invite me in?"

Her eyebrow arched. "For what reason?"

"So I can say hello to your aunt."

"Sorry, she's asleep and I don't want to wake her up."

He managed to smile. Boy, she was stubborn. "And I wouldn't want you to. Considering everything, I'm sure she needs her rest." *Just like considering everything, I think you're trying to hide the desire that's so blatant in your eyes, in the hard tips of your nipples that are pressing against your blouse. Why are you fighting me?*

"Thanks for delivering the flowers."

Natalie's voice intruded into his thoughts, and acting on pure impulse, he moved a step closer to her. The only thing separating their bodies was the vase of flowers she held in her hand. He wanted to get a clear view of the look in her eyes, to see what she wasn't yet experienced enough to hide. An image came back into his mind, the one of finding her asleep in his bed.

But in this one, she wasn't fully clothed. Instead she was stark naked.

He released a sharp intake of breath, and at that moment he was more determined than ever to have her, to do all those things to her he had dreamed about last night and envisioned most of the day.

"Goodbye, Mr. Steele."

As incredible as it was at that point in time, a slow smile formed on his lips. For now he would let her assume she was calling the shots. His smile widened even more as he took in her obvious apprehension. No doubt she was concerned just what his sudden good mood was about. Especially when the air surrounding them was shrouded with so much sensuality. It was so thick he could probably wallow in it. He felt it and knew she could feel it too.

"Please let your aunt know that I dropped by," he said in a husky yet hushed tone before taking a step back.

Without giving her time to say anything—and doubting seriously that she would have done so anyway—he turned and walked away.

Chapter 5

"What do you know about Donovan Steele, Farrah?" Natalie asked her friend as she watched her check her side mirrors before changing lanes. They were on their way to the Racetrack Café for an evening of fun.

At the first opportunity she could grab, Farrah glanced over at her. "Donovan Steele?" she asked with surprise in her voice. "Why on earth would you ask about him?"

Because maybe talking about him will stop my breasts from aching whenever I think about him. She had literally been in one hell of a fix since seeing him yesterday. She hadn't expected him to drop by, nor had she expected her body's reaction to seeing him. "I'm just curious."

She figured that response would not be good enough for Farrah and wasn't surprised to find herself under Farrah's intense stare when they came to a flashing light at the train tracks.

"No, girlfriend, you're not just curious," Farrah said. "You just got back in town last week, so why would you be asking about Donovan Steele?"

Natalie squirmed under Farrah's intense scrutiny and knew she would have to tell her the whole story since Farrah wouldn't let up until she did. "He's one of Aunt Earline's clients, and I was cleaning his home on Monday when he came home unexpectedly."

"Um, so you got to see the handsome hunk?" Farrah asked smiling as she waited for a train to pass.

"Unfortunately, I did. But that's not all I did,"

Farrah lifted her brow. "What else did you do?"

"I was cleaning his room, saw his bed, saw how comfortable it looked and wanted to try it out."

Farrah's eyes widened. "You got in Donovan Steele's bed, the one upstairs?"

Not understanding why the location of the bed would make a difference, Natalie shamefully admitted. "Yes. I was just going to try out the mattress to see if it was as soft as it looked. I hadn't intended on falling asleep."

"You actually fell asleep?" Farrah laughed. "Wow, that's rich."

"I don't know about it being rich since he found me there."

"Let me get this straight," Farrah said, wiping tears of laughter from her eyes. "You fell asleep in Donovan Steele's bed and he found you there?"

"Yes."

Farrah shook her head. "I'm sure your aunt hated losing him as a client."

"She didn't. As a matter of fact, he increased his cleaning service from twice a month to every week," Natalie informed her.

Farrah didn't say anything, but Natalie could see her friend's mind at work. She was working out everything Natalie had told her in her head to come up with a reason for Donovan Steele's action. Natalie could have saved her the trouble. She wasn't born yesterday, nor was she the naive, brainy professor some men thought she was. She knew exactly what his motives were.

"He wants you," Farrah finally said matter-of-factly.

"Yes, that's what I figured, especially since he thinks I'm no more than a cleaning lady. I didn't bother telling him what I really did for a living."

Farrah smiled. "So, you're going to try him out?"

Natalie looked aghast. "Of course not! I know his true colors since he's been taking every opportunity to display them. I hear from Aunt Earline that he's Charlotte's number one player, and there is no doubt in my mind that he's looking for another conquest. I have no intentions of being the next notch on his bedpost."

Farrah didn't say anything for a moment, and Natalie had a feeling when her friend did speak again that she wouldn't like whatever she would say.

"You may want to reconsider that decision, Nat. A fling with him might give you a new attitude," Farrah said softly.

Natalie knew that look, and once again she squirmed accordingly. While in high school, the only time she put her books aside to indulge in some honest to goodness, off-the-wall fun was when Farrah talked her into it. Otherwise, she would have lived a relatively boring life. But this was not their school days and Farrah, who'd been thrust back into the life of a swinging single, evidently wanted her to join her.

"Don't look at me like that, Farrah. I know what you're thinking."

Farrah then gave her that smile she knew so well. "And what am I thinking?"

"That I need to take advantage of it because it's been years since I got laid." Natalie knew there was nothing Farrah could say but confirm her statement since recently that had been Farrah's constant argument. Over the years, Farrah had relentlessly tried building the case that Natalie needed to get her head out of her books and stop spending so much time in the lab and work on another type of formula—one that produced a love life, and if not a *serious* love life, definitely a fling.

"Yes, that's what I'm thinking and it makes perfect sense, don't you think?" Farrah interrupted her thoughts by saying.

Natalie rolled her eyes heavenward. "No, that's not what I think."

"Come on, Nat, what do you have to lose? You don't know what you're missing out on. You can't convince me you aren't curious."

Natalie wished she could deny what Farrah was saying but she couldn't. She hadn't slept with anyone since college and Karl. Only Farrah knew the full extent of the scars a man's emotional abuse could leave. But she had tried moving on, only to encounter men who weren't cunning and manipulative like Karl but who were weak-minded enough to feel threatened by a woman's successful scholarly achievements.

"Look, Nat," Farrah said, after glancing at the car in front of them to make sure it hadn't moved. "Seriously. I'm not saying you need to start sleeping around, by any means. All I'm saying is that you should enjoy your life and not give in to the failures of the only man you've ever slept with by thinking all men are that way."

Natalie knew she didn't think that way, but she would be the first to admit one of the reasons she hadn't been hitting the singles scene was because she felt more comfortable in her career than in the prospect of putting all that work into a relationship to nowhere.

When Farrah checked on the cars ahead of them again, Natalie decided not to let her off the hook so easily. "What about you, Farrah? Did Dustin make you think all men are that way?" Natalie studied Farrah's features. She saw a glimpse of the pain in her friend's eyes that was still there even after a full year.

"I'm trying to move on, Nat. And no, I don't think all men are like Dustin, but I will admit the next one who comes close to my heart will have a tough job convincing me that he's not. In other words, no man will ever capture my heart again."

Natalie knew Farrah meant every word she had spoken. To this day Natalie didn't understand how

Dustin could have hurt Farrah the way he had. Regretting she had brought him up, she steered the conversation back to what she'd asked Farrah earlier.

"So, are you going to tell me what you know about Donovan Steele?" The cars started moving ahead, and she watched as Farrah shifted the car back in gear.

"Not much to tell. I've seen him before at a charity function or two so I know he's an extremely good-looking man. I only know what I read and what I overhear from the women at the gym. According to them, he only indulges in short-term affairs and is very selective about whom he sleeps with. Some women think it's quite an honor to be the chosen one because he's one hell of a lover."

Farrah glanced over at her when the car stopped at a traffic light. "I also hear he's very persuasive and could probably talk the panties off a nun."

Natalie couldn't help but smile at that claim. "All the more reason to keep him at arm's length," she said.

She could see him as a persuasive guy since if given the chance he would have tried wearing down her resistance on Tuesday evening. Hadn't he told her he went after whatever he wanted and always succeeded in getting it? He'd given her fair warning. And she planned on taking it.

"We're here."

Natalie was pulled out of her thoughts to glance through the car window. The parking lot was full. "This place gets a lot of business, I gather."

Farrah smiled. "Yes, I've only been here once before with a girl from work. The food was good and the entertainment even better. And since you aren't interested in having a fling with Donovan Steele, I'm sure you'll meet some other likable guy here."

Natalie rolled her eyes. Having a fling was the last thing she was interested in.

"You want another beer, Donovan?"

"No, thanks. I'm fine, Jon. I'll be checking out in a few," Donovan said, sparing the bartender a quick glance before returning his gaze back to the flat-screen television on the wall behind the counter. They were showing a rerun of last weekend's race in New Hampshire.

When the bartender moved on, Donovan leaned back against the barstool accepting the fact that his full concentration wasn't on the race. Instead, over the course of the night, as well as the nights before, he had done a very unorthodox thing. He had allowed a woman to dominate his thoughts.

He wasn't sure how to view his meeting with Natalie when he had delivered the flowers. She'd been feisty—that was for sure. And strong-willed. But he had a feeling she was also a very passionate woman. And it was that passion he would love to get a hold on and work to his advantage. Last night he had dreamed about her. In sleep he had inhaled her scent, imagined her legs wrapped around him and envisioned her lips mingling with his.

He had awakened with sweat covering most of his body and an erection as hard as a rock. He was glad to see the work week come to an end and was looking forward to the weekend. He had a date lined up with

Jean Carroll and he knew from past experiences that she would make it worth his while.

He happened to glance back up at the television screen and then looked to the mirror on the wall that picked up a clear view of anyone walking through the restaurant's door. He blinked thinking he was seeing things, but when he continued to stare at the mirror he saw that Natalie and another woman had come through the door. He was tempted to turn around but knew if he did she would definitely see him. So, instead, he sat there and watched as a waitress led them over to the table and out of sight.

Releasing the breath he'd been holding, he caught Jon's eye and beckoned him over to him.

"Another beer?" Jon asked.

Donovan shook his head. "No, but you see the two women Marisa just seated at a table in the back. I want you to give them whatever they want."

Jon strained his neck to see who Donovan was talking about. "Okay. Will you be joining them?"

"Later."

"All right." Jon then walked off.

Donovan pulled in a deep breath. What he didn't tell Jon was he wouldn't go anywhere near that table until he got himself together. He couldn't believe Natalie was here, invading his domain. It was bad enough he'd thought of little else besides her all day; now she was going to give him a reason to think of her all night. Again. And now there was a slow burn in his belly, and he seriously doubted even a cold beer would be able to put it out.

He glanced back at the television screen, trying to

ignore the fact she was there, but everything in front of him seemed to blur while a current of electricity seemed to charge the air.

Donovan glanced at his watch as heat flowed through his midsection. It was barely eight and too early for him to think about going home. And why should he? He had never ducked the other way when it came to a woman. Goldilocks had once again invaded his turf, so the way he saw it he had rights— rights he intended to exercise. He had given her fair warning.

Getting off the stool, he headed in her direction.

"Everything on the menu looks good," Natalie said to Farrah. "What are you going to have?"

"Um, that guy who just walked in looks pretty good."

Natalie glanced up, followed Farrah's gaze and nodded in agreement. "Yes, he does look good but, unfortunately, he's not on the menu."

"What a shame. I wish he was."

Natalie chuckled, but her laughter was cut short when she saw the man in question approached by another man. "I don't believe it," she said in an annoyed voice.

Farrah, who had gone back to studying her menu, glanced up. "You don't believe what?"

"Donovan Steele is here, and he's talking to your guy—the one you wished was on the menu. Hopefully, he won't look over this way and see me."

As if those very words had damned her, Donovan glanced her way. His gaze settled on her face and held her eyes captive. She barely had time to draw in a ragged breath when she felt white-hot desire whisk through her veins and settle deep in her limbs. So deep she had to place her glass of water back down on the table.

"Natalie?"

She heard Farrah call her name but was too caught up in the intensity of Donovan's gaze to break eye contact. She finally answered nonetheless. "Yes?"

"Are you sure you told me everything about your relationship with Donovan Steele?"

That question made Natalie meet Farrah's curious expression. She swallowed deeply. "Yes." When Farrah continued to look at her, she finally asked in a strained voice, "What do you think I didn't tell you?"

"How much you want to jump his bones."

Hearing Farrah speak aloud what she had refused to acknowledge in her thoughts caused a blush to color her cheeks. Did she really want to do that? Was that the reason why every morning since meeting him she'd waken with sensuous aches in her body and dreams too scandalous to mention to anyone?

"Natalie?"

She knew she had to say something or Farrah wouldn't let up. "I plead the fifth."

Farrah chuckled. "You can plead the fifth all you like, but it's not going to help you since both men are headed this way."

Natalie refused to turn her head to see if Farrah was teasing her. She knew she wasn't. There was no way for her and Donovan Steele to be in the same place without him trying to use his power of persuasion on her. "Remember what I said. He doesn't know what I actually do for a living and I want to keep it that way," she whispered.

Farrah smiled. "I'll keep your secret, but from the way he's looking at you, I doubt what you do for a living is what's on his mind right now."

Natalie couldn't resist temptation any longer, and she shifted her gaze to see the two men walking toward them. Farrah was right.

Xavier Kane glanced over at Donovan. "Hey, man, are you sure those ladies don't mind being interrupted?"

Donovan smiled as they kept walking toward where Natalie and a friend were sitting. He liked Xavier. Known as X, he was a close friend and personal attorney to the man who'd married his cousin Vanessa last year, Cameron Cody, and was the godbrother to Donovan's friend from college, Uriel Lassiter.

"We'll find out soon enough, X. Doesn't she look happy to see us coming?"

X chuckled. "Depends on which one you're focused on."

"I've got my eye on the one in blue. We have a little matter we need to resolve."

X let out a sigh of relief. "That's good because she's the one shooting daggers at us. I'm glad I'm focused on the other one. She's smiling. I can work with that smile. All I have to do is turn up the heat."

As Donovan got closer to the table, he decided regardless of the cold look Natalie was sending his way, he intended to turn up the heat, as well.

Chapter 6

"How are you tonight, Natalie?"

She would be a lot better if he didn't seem to be in such a good mood. He was smiling, and his white teeth against his creamy cocoa complexion made his smile even sexier. And then there was the sound of his voice—throaty, husky, just enough to feel like a caress across her heated skin. This man had the ability to stir every nerve-tingling sensation in her body and was doing so. Probably intentionally.

"I'm fine." And then she asked, "What are you doing here?"

He chuckled. "I could ask you the same thing since this is my hangout. I'm here every Friday night unless I'm out of town. My best friend is one of the owners. Considering all of that, it's my turn to ask. What are you doing here?"

Telling herself it would serve no purpose to argue with him, she glanced over at Farrah and quickly recalled her manners. "I'm here with my friend from high school. Farrah, this is Donovan Steele."

Donovan quickly took up the introductions by taking the hand Farrah offered him and said, "It's nice meeting you, Farrah, and I would like the both of you to meet a friend of mine, Xavier Kane."

Pleasantries were exchanged and handshakes were made. "Do you mind if we join you?" Donovan asked.

Natalie was about to say yes, she did mind, but Farrah spoke first. "No, of course not. We'd love for the two of you to join us."

Donovan, Natalie noted, was already pulling out a chair before Farrah had finished issuing the invitation. She also noted that he took the chair closer to her while Xavier sat beside Farrah.

"So, have you ladies ordered yet?" Xavier asked, smiling at everyone but especially at Farrah.

"No, we were checking out the menu. We've never been here before so what do you guys suggest?" Farrah asked. Farrah glanced over at her, and Natalie merely raised an arched brow—her way of sending a silent message that she was not happy. Instead of being bothered by her soundless threat, Farrah merely smiled sweetly over at her, and at that moment Natalie knew Farrah was up to something. That had her worried.

"Since you asked," Donovan said, "for appetizers I would suggest their coconut shrimp if the two of you like seafood."

"We do," Farrah quickly spoke up for the both of them. "And especially shrimp."

Donovan smiled. "Then you're in luck because for the main course it's all the fried shrimp you can eat tonight. They also have a variety of other seafood dishes that are just as delicious."

Natalie pretended to concentrate on the menu. Out of the corner of her eye she saw that Donovan had leaned back in his chair as if listening to the getting-to-know-you conversation between Farrah and Xavier. He was also pretending, because she was fully aware his attention was focused on her.

"How is your aunt?" he asked.

His question made her glance at him over the top of the menu, and she wished she hadn't. Tonight he was sitting under a light fixture that seemed to high-light all those features she had tried forgetting this week but had found herself dreaming about anyway. He had a beautiful pair of eyes. She had noticed them before, but for the first time she allowed herself time to literally drown in their dark depths.

"She's fine. Thanks for asking," she heard herself say before returning her attention back to the menu. Suddenly feeling hot, she reached for her cold glass of water and took a sip.

"Better?"

She glanced over at him again. "Excuse me?"

He smiled. "I asked if you felt better. Did the water quench your thirst? Cool you off?" he leaned over closer and asked silkily.

She stiffened at the underlying assumption. Okay, it was true that she was hot but not necessarily in the way he assumed. Although he was probably right. "As a matter of fact, yes, I do feel better."

At that moment the waitress returned to take their order, and Natalie had a feeling before the night was over she would be drinking plenty of cold water.

Given the way that he and Natalie had parted on Tuesday, if anyone would have told them that on Friday night they would be sitting next to each other sharing a meal he would not have believed them.

She didn't have a lot to say; her friend was the talkative one. She seemed satisfied just to eat and listen. And he was content just to sit and watch her. She was affecting him more than he'd ever imagined any woman capable of doing. In a way that bothered him; actually it frustrated the hell out of him.

The only reason he could come up with for his obsession was the fact that he'd found her in his bed. The same bed no other woman had ever lain in. Relying on his memory of those psych classes he'd taken in college, he knew there had to be an underlying meaning, a valid connection, between his fixation and her in his bed. His theory? She'd stepped into a part of his space that no other woman had ever invaded, and because of it, he was determined to get her back in that bed.

Whatever the reason, it really didn't matter, he inwardly conceded, taking a sip of his beer. Natalie Ford was in his system, buried deep, and he only knew one way to get her out. It was only then that he could move on to other things—specifically, other women. Until then…

"So, your best friend is one of the owners of this place," she said as if finally deciding to make small

talk. Xavier and Farrah had just excused themselves
to go to the game room to shoot some pool, leaving
them alone. He could tell by the way she'd glared at
her friend that she hadn't wanted to be left alone with
him.

He met her gaze, held it a moment and then said,
"Yes. He and several other race car drivers. I would in-
troduce you to Bronson but he left this morning for
Florida."

To pursue a woman, Donovan thought, shaking his
head. Bronson was the one man he'd figured would
never do something as crazy as chasing after a woman,
but he'd been proven wrong. No one had really been
surprised when Myles Joseph had gotten married
earlier that year. After all, they'd heard for years about
the woman Myles had left behind in Florida but who
still had his heart. But for Bron, a man who could
basically have any woman he wanted, to willingly
settle on just one—especially one determined not to
even give him the time of day—had shocked the hell
out of Donovan mainly because Bronson used to be
an even more devout player than he was.

She must have felt him staring at her and looked up.
A sensuous flutter automatically traveled up his spine.
At the same time he was aware of the slight shiver that
touched her body although she didn't know he'd seen
it. A man as experienced and well-versed in women
as he was didn't miss too much of anything.

The lighting in this particular section of the restaurant was low, and her features, especially her eyes,
seemed more profound in the candlelight gleaming
from the table.

He wondered if they were playing a game, a test of wills, to see who could hold whose gaze the longest. Who would be the first to look away? If that was the case, they could sit here all night. He was a master at seduction, and for her he intended to be on top of his game.

"Are you sure you don't want to go join X and Farrah in the game room?"

She tilted her head but didn't shift her gaze. "I don't know how to play."

"It's not hard. I could teach you. Give you a quickie."

The moment he'd said the word *quickie* he felt the lower part of his body harden, felt a spark ignite in his gut. And he could tell she'd also picked up on that single word, although she'd tried keeping all traces of a reaction from her face. But he had seen the slight widening of her eyes. He had heard her sharp intake of breath and had locked in on the judicious quivering of her lips. He didn't have her just where he wanted her by any means, but he knew his play on words was getting to her, would eventually break down her resistance. But first he had to calm her fears about being uncomfortable with him, while at the same time continuing to let her know where he stood and exactly what he wanted. Suddenly his mind was filled with all those lovemaking positions he had jotted down on a piece of paper earlier in the week.

He took a sip of his beer, licked his lips and still holding her gaze asked, "So, Natalie, are you interested in learning something new?"

Natalie's mouth tightened at the challenge since that's exactly what she saw his question as. Heaven help her, but she was seriously giving his suggestion some thought. Not that she would do anything other than let him teach her how to play pool, of course. But she was very well aware that his mind was on something else. She knew a play on words when she heard it, and if he thought he would get the better of her, he had another thought coming.

"It depends on what I'm learning and who's doing the teaching," she finally replied.

Was it her imagination or did his eyes just darken? Either way, she suddenly fought a tightening in her stomach and a warm feeling between her legs. She broke eye contact with him long enough to reach for her glass of water to take a cool refreshing sip. At the moment, she didn't care what he was thinking.

"What if I promise to make any training session worth your while? And it doesn't have to be learning how to play pool. Is there anything you want to learn how to do for the first time or learn how to do better?" he asked, his voice deep, strong and quietly seductive.

While deep longing and need seemed to wrap her in their strong embrace, Natalie studied his eyes with the same intensity that he was studying hers. She could not deny that something was building inside of her, an urgency she wasn't familiar with or used to.

Her eyes shifted from his eyes to his lips—full, sexy and kissable. It was then she remembered something that Karl had once told her; she couldn't kiss worth a damn. It had only been his opinion but it had still hurt, and she hadn't felt inclined to kiss another man for fear of him rendering that same verdict. Karl's remarks about her kisses had been rather kind compared to the score he'd given her lovemaking skills.

"Tell me," he repeated, his tone remarkably patient, "is there something you wish to learn how to do or learn to do better?"

Natalie swallowed. She had to regain control of her senses or else she would be spilling her guts to him, telling him about every deficiency Karl claimed she had and asking him to prove her ex-lover wrong. Further complicating matters, she would probably go as far as asking him to disprove some men's belief that a woman who possessed a high IQ was nothing more than an intellectual geek who didn't have a sensuous bone in her body.

For one instant she was tempted, but then she realized her limitations with this man. He wanted an affair, which was something she could very well do without. That pushed her to say, "No, there's nothing new I want to learn and nothing I want to improve at, although that doesn't mean I'm perfect in everything."

He continued to look at her as if he was trying to read her mind. "If you're sure…"

"I am."

"All right, but if you ever change your mind, let me know."

She opened her mouth to tell him that wouldn't be happening when Xavier and Farrah returned to the table. She could tell by the smile on her friend's face that she was enjoying Xavier's company.

"Who won?" she asked.

Farrah made a face. "He did, of course. But I think I surprised him."

Xavier laughed. "You most certainly did."

At that moment music from the live band began playing, and before Farrah could settle into her seat, Xavier had captured her hand and was pulling her back to her feet. "Come on, let's dance."

"All right," Farrah said smiling and off they went.

"Let's not allow them to outdo us this time," Donovan said, pushing his chair back and standing up.

Natalie stretched her neck to look up at him. The band was performing a slow number, and she wasn't sure it would be a good idea for them to dance together. The thought of their bodies connecting, rubbing against each other, while the smooth, often sensuous melody of slow music surrounded them was too much to consider.

She opened her mouth to decline when he held out his hand to her. "Don't be afraid of me, Natalie."

His tone was quiet, not challenging nor mocking. There was no way she could explain to him that at the moment her emotions were too strong for a slow dance. "I'm not afraid of you, Mr.—"

"No, not tonight. I am not Mr. Steele tonight, or are you afraid to call me Donovan?"

"I'm not afraid of anything," she said drawing in a controlling breath.

"Then prove it."

A part of her felt she didn't have to prove anything to him, but another part knew she had to prove something to herself. It had taken her months to get over Karl's mental abuse, to build up her self-esteem. She would be the first to admit that other than her co-workers at the university, her students, her professional affiliations and the few neighbors she'd gotten to know, she basically lived a solitary life, and in a few years she would be turning thirty with no plans to change the way she existed.

So, she would get through this dance not for him but for herself. With that thought in mind, she placed her hand in his. The moment their hands touched there was a spontaneous reaction. Fire and passion seemed to rush through her veins and settle in every finger in her hand. She made an attempt to pull her hand away but he held it in a tight grip.

She recalled very little about crossing the room to the dance floor or the smirk she saw on Farrah's face. But she did remember the exact moment Donovan pulled her into his arms, settled her against his rock-solid muscular form to bury her body into his heat and his scent.

He wrapped his arms around her waist, and she instantly responded and then tried to bring some semblance of control to the clamoring going on inside her body. As if it belonged there, her head automatically settled against the firmness of his chest.

A warning alarm went off in her head, a warning she decided not to heed. She rarely stole moments for herself to just chill and relax, enjoy the moment. She'd never taken time to enjoy a man. However, she intended to do so now.

She closed her eyes not wanting to think. Instead she allowed her mind and her senses to drink in the perfection of this moment on the dance floor in the arms of a man who was as handsome as handsome could get.

And he was caring, although such a depiction might be stretching it a bit. For all she knew, his current show of tenderness was just part of his ploy to get inside her panties. But still, the large hand gliding softly across her back was tumbling her into a myriad of sensations and feelings she hadn't counted on. For the moment, she didn't have to think about her class load for the fall and how many lab projects she would have to assign. The only thing she wanted to think about was the here and now in Donovan Steele's arms.

It didn't take long for the music to stop, and with the ending came the return of her senses. She lifted her head from his chest and retreated a step, noting he kept a firm hand on her back. "Let's take a walk," he suggested softly.

"A walk?"

At his nod, she asked, "Where?"

"Outside. For just a minute. I need to catch some fresh air."

She was about to tell him that he didn't need her to go with him to catch some fresh air, but the hand in the center of her back was propelling her forward, through the double doors that led out back. The moment their feet touched the porch, he turned her into his arms to face him.

The moment she looked up into his eyes, she knew. And it had nothing to do with getting fresh air but had everything to do with him getting her.

Donovan tried drawing in a controlling breath and knew it was a waste of time. As calm as he might have looked, he was totally out of control. And he placed the blame solely at Natalie's feet. He wasn't sure if it was the way she was dressed, in a pair of snug-fitting jeans that were molded to her hips and to her backside with flawless precision and the white blouse that had a few buttons undone to show the rounded curve of her full breasts. Or it could have been the perfume she was wearing that made his body think of hot sex every time he sniffed it. But then it could have been the way she was wearing her hair, pulled back in a cute ponytail with ringlets of curls crowning her face. He felt a naughty urge to remove that rubber band from her hair to see it tumble around her shoulders and then run his fingers through the lustrous locks.

Those were just some of the reasons his heart was now beating erratically in his chest and he had an erection. They were also the reasons his tongue felt thick in his mouth, filled with a greedy desire to mate with hers.

But the main reason he was in such a bad way was how she'd felt in his arms and how with every sway of her hips against him he'd had to take a steadying breath—and each breath only intensified his desire for her. So now, although he was fighting like hell to remain calm, he was feeling every amorous bone in his body tilting over the edge. And it wasn't helping matters the way she was looking up at him, with an expression that said she was waiting for him to do something, even though she didn't have a clue what he'd be doing.

Deciding not to keep her in suspense any longer, he lowered his head to hers, his lips delivering minimum pressure on hers, fighting back his desire to devour them to the full extent. He nibbled at her, used his tongue to lick the corners of her mouth over and over again.

And then under their own will, her lips parted, eased open slightly, enough for his own tongue to slip inside and claim her mouth fully with a possessiveness that had him moaning deep in his throat. And then he confronted something else he knew that would do him in. Her taste.

He felt his erection throb. He felt the tips of her nipples press hard against his shirt, and immediately his hand went into action and drifted lower from her back and beyond the smallness of her waist to settle on the curve of her butt. Amazing and magnificent all rolled into one single piece of hot flesh.

He groaned again, and the tone of the kiss changed. He became greedy as sensations washed through him, sensations he felt all the way down to his toes. He heard her sexy little moan, and he couldn't help wondering how it would feel to share an orgasm with her. To ease his throbbing erection. To press the hard strength of his body inside her all the way to the hilt. To thrust into her with the same rhythm he was using on her mouth.

In his bed.

He wondered if he were to ask whether she would go home with him tonight, sleep in his bed, make love with him as many times as the two of them could handle. All night long sounded pretty damn good about now. With his hand on her backside he pressed her closer, knowing there was no way she could not feel his hard-on pressed against her stomach.

He slowly pulled his mouth away from hers but it didn't go far. It nibbled around her lips, kissed the corners of her mouth. "Natalie, come home with me tonight," he whispered hotly against her moist lips.

* * *

Natalie wasn't sure why she allowed Donovan to kiss her, why even now she wasn't resisting while he continued to kiss her, other than by doing so she was proving Karl wrong. If she couldn't kiss worth a damn like Karl had claimed then someone had forgotten to tell Donovan Steele. He appeared to enjoy locking lips with her as much as she was with him. If he hadn't liked it he wouldn't have let it last so long. He sure wouldn't be still messing around with her mouth the way he was, licking it, greedily nibbling on it like it was better than any candy he'd eaten. And it sure wouldn't have him hard to the extent that she could feel his aroused shaft pressing against the lower part of her.

But more than anything, he wouldn't be asking her to go home with him if she was such an awful kisser. However, she wouldn't be going anywhere with him since she wasn't fooled, not for a second, what he was all about. He wanted a wham, bam, thank you, ma'am, and unfortunately she didn't know the first thing about engaging in short, meaningless affairs. But then the one she thought was going to be a long, meaningful one with Karl had left a bad taste in her mouth...a bad taste she had to admit Donovan had just replaced with a pleasant one.

"Natalie."

He whispered her name again in this deep, husky voice that could make the area between her legs ache, make her panties get wet. She could barely resist the urge to reach out and undo his zipper and take that aroused part of him in her hand to see how the thickness would feel touching it.

How could she think of doing such a thing? She was actually contemplating playing out what her mind had dreamed several times. For the first time in years her body felt ravenous for a man.

Her lips parted with a groan. That was all the opening it seemed that he needed to slide his tongue back into her mouth in an attempt to kiss her into agreeing to go home with him. She wouldn't change her mind about it. But he could try.

And he did.

This time his lips were hard and demanding yet at the same time persuasive. So persuasive that she had to grip his shoulders to keep her knees from buckling beneath her. Never had she been kissed like this, being rendered helpless to do anything but to kiss him back.

At that moment the back door flew open and they quickly pulled apart and glanced over at the intruder. One of the cooks stood in the doorway with an apologetic look on his face. "Oops. Sorry. I just wanted to come out here to grab a smoke." And then just as quickly as he had appeared, he was gone back inside.

But his appearance had given her just enough time to clear her head and make her take a step back. She glanced up at Donovan, met his gaze and swallowed deeply. He had desire in his eyes, deep, dark, seductive, and she knew if she wasn't careful she would be falling under his spell.

"We need to go back inside, as well," she managed to say. "And I won't be going home with you tonight, Donovan." There, she'd said his first name. To call him Mr. Steele now wouldn't make much sense, especially after the torrid kiss they had just shared. So much for keeping things on a professional level. All she could do at this point was make sure things between them didn't escalate any further.

"Well, at least you're not calling me Mr. Steele anymore," he said, mimicking her very thoughts. "And you're sure you don't want to go home with me?"

She tilted up her chin, met his gaze. "Positive. I know when and where to draw the line."

A smile touched the corners of his mouth, and it was so magnetic she almost felt her lips being pulled in its direction. "And I know when and where to turn up the heat, Natalie," he countered.

There was no doubt in her mind that he did. Nor did she doubt that he would. "Donovan," she said, hearing his name a second time and trying to downplay how much she liked saying it. "I think we need to make some decisions."

He lifted a brow. "About what?"

"Whether I should remain your housekeeper. Like I said on Monday, we have a number of other ladies who can—"

"No. And if you're basing your suggestion on the kiss we've shared, forget it."

She glared up at him. "You're being difficult."

He raised what she thought was an arrogant brow and said, "Sweetheart, you've never met a Steele at a time when he's being difficult, and trust me, you wouldn't want to. What I'm being is realistic. I know what I want, just like I know what you want. If I didn't before, I do now. Your kiss said it all. Stroke for stroke. Lick for lick."

She tilted her head back and she knew that

defiance—in all its glory—was shining in her eyes. Fine! So she'd never met a Steele being difficult. Well, he was about to meet a Ford when she was. "I'm not one to act mainly on physical attraction. I will not be pushed into an affair with you."

He chuckled. "I don't plan to push, Natalie. I plan to seduce, and when I do, babe, you won't stand a chance."

Natalie inhaled a deep breath. In all her twenty-six years, she had never met a man quite like him. He actually thought he was all that. He figured all he had to do was snap his fingers and they would go tumbling between the sheets. Maybe that was how easy it had been for the other women he'd encountered, but he would see that she was cut from a totally different mold. Because of her mother's wild and reckless ways, she'd grown up with a very sensible mind. She'd done without sex for over five years and could very well do without for another five—even ten or twenty if she had to.

She was about to open her mouth to give him the dressing down that he deserved when he said, "No more arguing tonight, Natalie. Come on, let's go back inside."

A moment of indecision raced through her. Should she not argue anymore with him tonight and let him have the last word, or should she give a blistering retort? She had a feeling any type of rejoinder from her would fall on deaf ears. Besides, her aunt always said that with some people you have to show them rather than tell them. "Fine, let's go inside."

And without waiting for him to say anything, she headed for the door.

* * *

"Don't try and get tight-lipped on me now, Nat. What is going on with you and Donovan Steele?"

Natalie glanced over at Farrah. As soon as she had gotten back inside, she had waited only long enough for Farrah to return to the table from off the dance floor with Xavier to announce that she was ready to go.

"Trust me. You don't want to know," she said, glancing out the window at all the bright neon signs they were passing.

"Yes, I do. You tell me about you and Donovan, and I'll tell you about me and Xavier."

Natalie glanced back over at her. "Is there a *you* and Xavier?"

Farrah laughed. "Not the way you make it sound, no. Like I told you earlier tonight, after what Dustin did I won't ever let another man get close to my heart again."

Natalie nodded. "He seems nice."

"He is, but I was married to a nice man, remember? Or at least we thought he was nice. To some he might still be nice, but Dustin's main problem was that he didn't know how to keep his pants zipped for anyone but his wife."

The bitterness was still there in Farrah's voice, and Natalie wondered if it would ever go away. "Would you see Xavier again if he were to call you?" Natalie asked.

"Depends on the reason. If he calls because he's interested in a long-term affair then, no. But if he contacts me for a booty call, then maybe."

Natalie knew her friend actually felt that way, and

that was sad. Farrah had always been the dreamer, the one who wanted marriage and kids, the house with the white picket fence. The one who'd believed in forever after.

"But I won't have to worry about Xavier wanting to pursue anything serious," Farrah said. "I recalled hearing his name before and then I remembered where. He's one of those men in the Bachelors in Demand Club."

Natalie raised a brow. "What's the Bachelors in Demand Club?"

Farrah glanced over at her when the car came to a stop at a traffic light. "I heard some of the single women at work talking about it one day. It seems that years ago, six close friends from Morehouse made a pledge to each other the day before graduation that not only would they stay in touch but they would become godfathers to each other's children, and that the name of each of their first sons would begin with the letters U to Z. They kept their promise, and all six sons became godbrothers to each other. Most of them are now in their late twenties or early thirties. A few years ago, for some reason the six decided to form the Bachelors in Demand Club. In other words they are bachelors in demand, men who aren't interested in settling down until they've sown their wild oats, so to speak. Rumor has it that each of them·has his own heartbreak story to tell so now they intend to go through life making sure there isn't a repeat by guarding their heart."

Natalie pushed a curl out of her face and asked, "And you think Xavier is one of these men?"

"Pretty sure of it, but of course I didn't ask him about it to be certain. I do recall that there are two of them living in the Charlotte area, Xavier and a man by the name of Uriel Lassiter. The other four are spread out over the country."

Natalie didn't say anything for a moment and then she asked, "What do you think is Xavier's story?"

The traffic light changed to green and Farrah put the car in gear to begin moving. "Don't know his hang-ups, and I'm not going to worry about what they could be. In addition to being pleasing to the eyes, he was also great company tonight, but that's about it. He didn't suggest that we see each other again so I'm leaving it at that."

She quickly glanced back over at Natalie when traffic slowed again. "Enough talk about Xavier Kane. I want to know about you and Donovan and what went on when the two of you went out back."

Natalie rolled her eyes. Did Farrah not miss anything? "What do you think went on?"

"A quickie perhaps?" Farrah asked with a smirk.

Natalie couldn't help but grin. "No. Sorry to disappoint you."

"Heck, I bet the one who's really disappointed is Donovan Steele. When Xavier and I got back to the table and you announced that you were ready to leave, he actually looked like he could throttle you."

"Whatever."

"At least I know he kissed you," Farrah said, grinning. "And real good."

Natalie frowned. "And how do you know that?"

Now it was Farrah's time to roll her eyes. "Good

grief, Nat. Take out your compact and look at yourself. Your lips are still swollen."

Not knowing whether Farrah was teasing or serious, Natalie took out compact and looked at herself in the mirror. "Oh," she said, touching her lips while at the same time feeling a tint of embarrassment touch her cheeks.

"Yes, oh," Farrah said smiling. "But don't worry. Your aunt will probably be asleep when you get home tonight and your lips will be back to normal in the morning."

Natalie closed her compact wondering what Xavier Kane had thought. What had anyone thought who'd seen her lips? Probably the same thing Farrah thought. She had been well and truly kissed. And they were all right. Donovan had kissed her in a way she had never been kissed before and had made her feel things that until tonight had been foreign to her.

"Will you be seeing Donovan again, Nat? So he can kiss you again?"

Natalie tried ignoring the flash of pleasure that shot through her body at that possibility. "That was our first and last kiss. I won't be going out with him, which means the only time we could possibly see each other is when I'm there to clean his house. But those are the days he'll be at work, and I plan to get in and out before he comes home."

"Good luck, Nat."

Natalie glanced over at Farrah. "And why are you wishing me luck?"

"Because I think you're going to need it. You asked me what I know about Donovan, and I didn't finish telling you everything. What I didn't say that I've heard is that he's a man who gets whatever he wants, and tonight the look on his face made it pretty clear that he wants you."

Chapter 7

"Hey, man, you weren't at the top of your game today. What's up with you?"

Donovan shot his brother a frown. "There's nothing wrong with me Morgan, so get off my ass."

Bas dropped down on one of the bleachers and took a huge gulp from his water bottle, and then said, "Sounds like we might need to play another game since that one didn't seem to work out your frustrations, Don."

Donovan glared at his brothers, all three of them. It was a tradition that they play basketball at the gym every Saturday morning to work off any competitive frustrations that might have built up that week. For the four competitive adult males it was their way of not butting heads Monday through Friday at SC.

As much as Donovan didn't want to admit it, Morgan was right. He hadn't been at the top of his game. And it was all Natalie Ford's fault. There was no reason the woman should not have slept with him last night. No reason at all.

"Do you think we need to play another game for your benefit, Donovan?"

Chance's question interrupted Donovan's musings. He glared at his oldest brother. "No."

"Good, because I need to get home and get Alden," Chance responded glancing down at his watch. "Kylie is hosting a baby shower for Lena and Jocelyn, so Alden and I are getting lost for a while."

"Can I get lost with the two of you?" Morgan asked grinning.

"Include me in," Bas readily said. He glanced over at Donovan. "What about you, kid? You want to hang around with a bunch of happily married men?"

"No, I have better things to do with my time. Things married men only dream about doing," Donovan said, using a towel to wipe the sweat off his face.

"Don't be so sure of that, Donovan," Chance said grinning. "We hate to disappoint you, but married men can have just as much fun with their wives as single men have with their girlfriends—probably even more. Why is it that we, the married Steeles, are the ones in a good mood today, while you're the one who still needs a frustration adjustment? Doesn't sound to me like your girlfriend is doing her job."

Donovan's eyes narrowed. "I don't have a girlfriend."

"Hmm, then maybe you should consider getting

one," Chance threw over his shoulder as he, Bas and Morgan headed into the locker room, leaving Donovan glaring at their backs.

Donovan stared at the phone for a moment after hanging it up. He could not believe that he had just broken a date with Jean Carroll of all women. Jean, the one who came ready with her own set of handcuffs. And it was Natalie Ford's fault.

Ever since he had kissed her last night, his mind and body had started playing tricks on him. First, he had awakened after a night of dreaming about Natalie with a hard-on that wouldn't go away, even after he'd relieved his bladder and taken a cold shower. He had finally gotten it to act right by the time he had slipped into a T-shirt and jogging pants to meet his brothers for a game of basketball.

Then it had been the taste of her in his mouth that wouldn't fade. He had brushed his teeth, gargled several times and still whenever he smacked his lips he could taste her—that sweet, sensuous taste that had electrified his mouth while kissing her.

And lastly, it was the way she had felt in his arms, how soft and cuddly her butt had felt beneath the palms of his hands. He didn't want to touch another woman quite that way any time soon. His erection was throbbing for just one woman. If he didn't know better he'd think Natalie had cast a spell on him.

He was about to get up and head toward the kitchen when the phone rang. He checked the caller ID to make sure it wasn't Jean calling him back to try and change his mind about their date tonight. He sighed in relief when he saw it was his roommate and friend from college, Uriel Lassiter. Over the years, he and Uriel had maintained a close relationship.

He picked up the phone. "Uri, how are things going, man?"

"I'm still tired from last weekend at the races, but I called to give you some good news."

"What?"

"That publishing company in Colorado that we had our eye on last year is back on the market."

Donovan rubbed his chin thoughtfully. "Hmm, so what do you think?"

Uri chuckled. "I think that if you're still interested, I'll have an updated portfolio on your desk by Monday morning."

"Hey, that'll work because I'm still interested." His cousin Taylor was his wealth-asset manager and she was doing a fantastic job of managing his finances, but right out of college he and Uri had formed their own co-op. They'd started out flipping houses, and it became such a moneymaker that they expanded and began buying small companies and reselling them for a profit. The co-op had become so successful that they had invited a few select others to join in over the years. Uri had left his job as an insurance executive to handle the business end of things on a full-time basis.

Donovan talked to Uri another fifteen minutes before they ended the call. Standing, he stretched his body before heading toward the kitchen to grab a bite to eat. For the first time in years, this was a Saturday night and he didn't have anything to do.

*** *

He gave her a slow, sexy smile as he moved toward the bed, his gaze moving over her naked body, seeing everything but zeroing in on the area between her legs. The nipples on her breasts automatically hardened and she released a deep breath. He was pretty potent if the size of his erection was anything to go by. And his muscular body was masculinity at its perfection.

She watched as he began to move closer and closer, and without waiting for him to join her on the bed, she pulled up and willingly went into his arms. Together they tumbled back onto the covers.

Natalie's eyes flew open as she inhaled a long, deep breath. She'd just had another dream about Donovan. She couldn't believe she was letting him interrupt her sleep this way. Typically, she wasn't a hot and bothered woman, but there was something about Donovan that unleashed a sexual desire she had never encountered before. Never before had she dreamt about a man making love to her. Or almost making love to her, she corrected, since so far in none of her dreams had they finished the act. She would always wake up moments before their bodies joined as one.

She inhaled deeply not sure if that was a good thing or a bad thing. In a way it was bad because she woke up curious as to how it would have been if they had. And it was a good thing because a part of her felt she really should not want to know.

But she did.

And that area between her legs was tingling to find out.

She glanced over at the illuminated clock on the nightstand. It was two in the morning.

Releasing a frustrated sigh, she pushed the covers aside and eased out of bed. She had brought her laptop with her to work on a few items for NASA while she was here. Last year she had received a national award for her work on stratospheric chemistry and ozone depletion. Her report had been embraced by the NASA Ames Research Center which had led to her working closely with the center last summer. Her findings had been put in a book that was doing quite well on the academic circuit. Now she was working again with NASA on a project to increase the rate of nitrous oxide in the atmosphere.

These studies had been her lifeline. When most people curled up at night with a good mystery novel, she much preferred curling up with her laptop to work on chemistry formulas. Very seldom did anything else consume her mind while working—definitely not the likes of any man. But Donovan Steele had somehow managed to seep inside the very essence of her brain that had always been off-limits. He had managed to invade a space that had always been kept reserved for all her subscripts. Somehow she needed to get back in sync.

Her aunt needed her so she didn't have the option to leave Charlotte. And she couldn't have her aunt drop him as a client because he headed the dependable list. He paid his bill on time and had few, if any, complaints or last-minute changes in the schedule that could cause the agency loss of revenue or manpower. In other words, he was a model client, one you didn't drop just because he intended to sleep with the cleaning lady's niece.

Of course, as far as she was concerned, it was wishful thinking on his part. But still, those dreams wouldn't go away. And to make matters worse, her conversation with Farrah last night still weighed heavily on her mind. It constantly reminded her that it had been years since she'd been intimate with someone and all because of one man.

At least Donovan had proven that Karl's kissing claim was wrong. Could he prove the other claims were wrong, as well? Was she as terrible in the bedroom as Karl had accused her of being?

As she sat down at the desk in the room and booted up her laptop, she couldn't help but inwardly call herself a fool for letting Karl mess with her confidence years ago.

Logging in to her Internet account, she went into the project folder that stored vital information when she wasn't on-site at the campus lab. And just in case someone tried hacking into her computer base, she had all the information coded in a way that only she could decipher. Usually when she worked on formulas she felt she was in her element. But tonight she knew deep down she was using her work as an escape.

In fact if she was completely honest with herself she would admit to having used it as a way of escaping for a very long time. At that moment she couldn't help but think about the vast differences between Karl and Donovan. Karl had been too brilliant for his own good and assumed because of his high IQ that everyone else was lacking. It had taken her years to realize that he hadn't been comfortable with his own skin, which was probably why he took great pride in downgrading others.

The complete opposite was true with Donovan. He was arrogant but he was also comfortable in his own skin. It was obvious that he was a man comfortable with who he was and what he represented. Manly, in and out.

Sensations flowed through her stomach when she thought about just how manly he was. That was what had her in a bad way. She had five days to get herself together. On Friday she would return to his home, and she wanted to make sure that she was in and out of there before he got in from work. She had six more weeks to go, and she intended to avoid the man at all costs.

"You're pregnant?" Donovan asked, looking into the smiling face of his cousin Vanessa. She had come into his office first thing Monday morning and dropped the bombshell, and he wanted to make sure he'd heard her correctly.

"Yes," she responded, bubbling all over with joy. "Cameron and I found out this morning. I'm sure Cameron has told Morgan already, and I talked to Mom, Taylor and Cheyenne on my way to work. But since Chance and Bas haven't arrived yet, you're the first here to know."

Feeling happy for his cousin, Donovan stood up and came from behind his desk to give her a huge hug. "I can imagine how happy Cam is," he said.

Vanessa smiled while at the same time wiped tears from her eyes. "He's extremely happy. I think we decided how much we both wanted a child the night we took on the role as babysitters for Little Dane," she said of her best friend Sienna's son. "He was such a joy, and we knew then we wanted a child of our very own."

"Let's just order up one baby this go-round, please," he said grinning. "I don't think the family will be able to handle it if you follow in Cheyenne's footsteps and have multiple babies." Vanessa's sister Cheyenne had given birth to triplets last year.

Vanessa chuckled. "Yes, but you have to admit Chey is doing a grand job with them along with Quade's help. I'm glad he convinced her to make North Carolina their home and use the house she owns in Jamaica as a vacation home."

Donovan nodded, thinking his brothers had all gotten married and now all of his girl cousins—at least the ones living here in Charlotte—were having babies. Taylor and Dominic's son had been born the first of the year.

"So when are you going to settle down, marry and start a family, Donovan?"

His answer was quick. "Never. I happen to like being single."

"I thought I did, too until I fell in love. So beware, your time is coming," she warned.

He frowned. "Don't hold your breath, sweetheart. Just glow in your own happiness and leave mine alone."

Vanessa studied his features. "But just think how much happier you could be curling up with the same person each night, someone who you loved."

"Love? I'll pass. There's not enough love in the world to make me fall in love with any woman."

KIMANI ROMANCE

An Important Message from the Publisher

Dear Reader,

Because you've chosen to read one of our fine novels, I'd like to say "thank you"! And, as a special way to say thank you, I'm offering to send you two more Kimani™ Romance novels and two surprise gifts – absolutely FREE! These books will keep it real with true-to-life African American characters that turn up the heat and sizzle with passion.

Please enjoy the free books and gifts with our compliments...

Glenda Howard

For Kimani Press

Peel off Seal and Place Inside...

FREE GIFTS
EDITOR'S SEAL
THANK YOU

We'd like to send you two free books to introduce you to Kimani Romance books. These novels feature strong, sexy women, and African-American heroes that are charming, loving and true. Our autho fill each page with exceptional dialogue, exciting plot twists, and enough sizzling romance to keep you riveted until the very end!

KIMANI ROMANCE ... LOVE'S ULTIMATE DESTINATION

Your two books have a combined cover price o $11.98, but are yours **FREE!** We'll even sen you two wonderful surprise gifts. You can't lose!

2 Free Bonus Gifts!

He went back around his desk and sat down, thinking that he was beginning to feel smothered by all these Steeles who were either getting married or having babies.

Chapter 8

Humming her favorite tune, Natalie unlocked the door to Donovan's home around nine o'clock Friday morning. She had called when she'd been a block away hoping he didn't answer, an indication that he'd left for work already. Her plan was to get in and out before noon just in case he decided to come home for lunch.

Placing her purse down on the sofa she moved toward the hall closet where he kept the cleaning supplies. She was in a good mood. Her aunt's visit to the doctor yesterday had gone well, and during Natalie's restless nights she had been able to finish the first part of the project she was working on with NASA.

She still had her nightly dreams and figured there

was no help for them. She was a woman whose needs were letting themselves known, but she was determined to ignore them like she always had, although they were more prevalent now than ever before.

She had finished cleaning the kitchen and had started in the living room, establishing her rhythm as she dusted the furniture while the sound of Ne-Yo blared through her earbuds. She liked music and enjoyed dancing, although her moves on Friday night had been different. She had been on the dance floor with Donovan, in his arms while moving to a slow tune. It had been a long time since she'd been held by a man that way. And even now she was experiencing aftershocks from when he'd taken her outside and kissed her, practically devouring her mouth.

Suddenly there was a tap on her shoulder. Startled, she yelped then spun around only to collide with a wide, solid chest. She jumped back, almost losing her balance in the process while placing her hand over her furiously beating heart. Donovan was standing there in bare feet and wearing a pair of jeans and a shirt that was completely unbuttoned and hung open showing a beautiful muscular chest. He looked as sexy as sin.

She snatched the earbuds from her ears as her gaze shifted from his face and moved lower to where a path of hair trailed from beneath his navel past the waistline of his jeans. She felt the heat of embarrassment rush to her cheeks when she looked back to his face and knew he was aware what area of his body had grabbed most of her attention.

Natalie wished he would button up his shirt and was tempted to suggest that he do so, but this was his house and he had the right to dress as he pleased. She swallowed, momentarily at a loss for words until she remembered he had just scared her out of her wits. She opened her mouth to speak, but he beat her to it.

"I tried to get your attention to let you know I was here, but you were too busy dusting and dancing around." He smiled. "And those were some pretty good moves, by the way."

She frowned, not in the mood for any of his humor. "What are you doing here, Donovan?"

A slow, deliberate smile touched his lips. "I live here."

She rolled her eyes. "Why aren't you at work?"

"I'm working at home today."

"Why?"

"Because I felt like it."

She wished she could throw her feather duster at him.

"I have a lot of work to do, and I promise to stay out of your way. The only reason I came downstairs was to grab a piece of fruit."

"So you won't be leaving for work today?" she asked.

"No."

"I wish you would have contacted the agency to let us know. We could have changed your cleaning to another day," she said.

"Why would you want to do that?"

She gave what she thought was an obvious answer. "You're here."

He lifted a brow. "Is that supposed to be a problem?"

She tilted her head while crossing her arms over her

chest, leveling him with her gaze before asking smartly, "What do you think?"

A rumble of a chuckle erupted from his throat. "I think you're making too much of it. I'm upstairs in my office out of your way, so you can skip that room today. I have work to do and I'm sure you do, as well."

Her eyes narrowed as she watched him turn and sprint up the stairs.

Donovan closed his office door behind him, leaned against it and let out a deep sigh. He was not accustomed to retreating from a woman that he wanted, a woman he intended to have. But Natalie had him rethinking his strategy, polishing his approach and modifying his tactics—and all with one final goal in mind. Seduction. He intended to get her back in his bed and make love to her, all day and all night. Only then would he effectively get her out of his system and move on.

With the Product Trade Show in a few months, he had too much work to do to let any one woman tie up his time with her continued rejections. He should be seducing her to his will, making love to her until he got enough, and once he got his fill he would walk away.

And not look back.

In the meantime, he would do whatever he had to do. If she thought she would eventually wear out his patience, then she was wrong. The woman had definitely underestimated his determination.

He drew in a deep breath. How could any one woman look so desirable? Those shorts and tank top she was wearing definitely weren't helping his libido. It was a different outfit from last week but it was hard for him to ignore just how good she looked in it. When he had come down the stairs and seen her move her body in a provocative dance while dusting, he had immediately gotten turned on. Hell, if he was totally honest with himself, he would admit that he had been turned on since waking up that morning and knowing that she would be coming today.

Now that she was here, the first thing he planned to do was break through her defenses. That was something he'd done Saturday night when they had shared a very intense kiss, a kiss that had blood rushing through his veins. A kiss that had kept him awake that night, fueling his lust.

Almost a week later and his lust was still getting fueled. Sighing again he went to sit behind his desk. He had brought work home. He had reports to read, and he had a conference call with Morgan and his research and development team in a half hour regarding Gleeve-Ware.

Donovan checked his watch. He would concentrate on work for a while, and then his full focus and attention would shift to Natalie.

Natalie was on her knees in the master bathroom, scrubbing the tile around the shower when she heard the door open to the office where Donovan had been sequestered for the past two hours.

She hoped if he was headed downstairs he wouldn't enter his bedroom but would keep moving down the stairs. She only had his bedroom left to clean and much preferred that he wasn't around while she did so, considering he'd found her asleep in his bed the last time she cleaned in here.

She listened to the steady footsteps and knew the moment he had entered the room and was standing there, in the open doorway, staring down at her. She might be imagining things, but she could feel the intensity of his gaze on her backside. So, let him look if that's what he wanted to do. She would just ignore him.

She tried. However, when seconds ticked into minutes and he didn't say anything, she shifted around, leaned back on her haunches and looked up at him. "Did you want something?"

She realized her mistake too late. The darkening of his eyes told her she was asking the one question better left unanswered. He evidently didn't agree and responded, "Yes."

Natalie swallowed deeply. She could just imagine what he wanted. The way he was looking at her said it all, but she knew the polite thing to do was to ask anyway, just in case she was wrong. After all, he was the client. "And how can I help you?" She grimaced thinking that question didn't sound much better.

"You can start off by getting off the floor. Does it really take all of that?" he asked.

His response wasn't what she expected, and she rolled her eyes, while at the same time trying to ignore how sexy he looked leaning in the doorway. "You're paying for cleaning services," she stated.

Donovan frowned. She didn't have to remind him, yet he still thought it didn't take all of that. He thought of how she'd looked on her knees with her backside tooted up in a cute way toward him. A tingle of desire had oozed through his stomach as if he hadn't been filled with wanting her already. It had been like adding kerosene to a flame already out of control when he thought about all the things he would like to do to that behind.

"Mr. Steele?"

His thoughts were pulled back at the sound of her voice. Then he concentrated on what she'd just called him. "You're starting that back up?"

"Starting what back up?"

"Calling me Mr. Steele."

"That's your name," she said, getting to her feet and pulling off the plastic gloves and tossing them into the trash can before washing her hands.

"For you, it's not. I'm Donovan. I thought we had straightened that issue out on Friday."

She dried her hands. "Had we?"

"I was certain that we had," he said, watching her put his cleaning supplies back under the cabinet and appreciating how she bent over to do so. He glanced around and sniffed the air. The placed looked clean and smelled good.

"Then I guess it's gone back to being business as usual," she said smartly, coming to a stop in front of him and tilting her head back to look up at him.

He wanted to show her just how wrong she was by pulling her into his arms and kissing that agitated look off her face.

"Excuse me."

It was then that he realized she needed to get by and expected him to move out of he way. It would have been the gentlemanly thing to do. But all he could think about was that his bed was less than six feet behind him, and he would love to take her over there, strip her naked and then make love to her.

"You want me to move?" he asked, knowing she did but liking her standing in front of him, closer than she even realized. Her scent was sensual and set off a flutter of desire in his stomach. And like Friday night, her hair was pulled back in a cute ponytail with ringlets of curls crowning her face.

On sudden impulse, he reached out, and with a flick of his wrist, while ignoring the look on surprise on her face he sent her hair tumbling around her shoulders.

"What do you think you're doing?" she asked, indignant.

Her indignation was something he could handle. What he couldn't handle—at least not much longer— was desiring her so much he could no longer think straight. His erection was growing heavier by the minute. "I just did something I was tempted to do Friday night. I wanted to see your hair tumble around your shoulders, and then I wanted to do this." He reached out and ran his fingers through the lustrous strands.

It was a bold move, and she stared up at him like he'd lost his mind. Maybe he had. While she seemed at a loss for words, totally stunned, he figured he might as well push the envelope and take things to another level.

On that decision, he lowered his mouth to hers and swept his tongue between her startled, parted lips. She moaned, which triggered his own groan, and his erection grew harder. Like the last time, this kiss was hot. It was also something desperate. Their tongues mingled and then began dueling, and in the process he felt his senses get shredded to pieces. When he felt her trembling, he wrapped his arms around her, needing to hold her as much as he wanted to believe she needed to be held.

He could tell she was too overtaken by the kiss to notice he was slowly walking backward, pulling her with him. And he continued to kiss her provocatively, without any restraints, not thinking of letting up and with a hunger that astounded him. He claimed her mouth with a free-for-all kiss as all those dreams that had tortured him this past week came surging back with megaforce. When the back of his legs touched his bed, he deepened the kiss and pulled her closer to him, gathered her tighter into his arms. Together they went tumbling backward, actually free-falling into the sheets.

But he didn't let up. In fact, knowing he had her where he wanted her actually made him sort of crazy, and it wasn't helping that she was responding to him with a passion that he felt all through his body.

He deepened the kiss to drown farther in the sweet recesses of her mouth, but that wasn't enough. He wanted to touch her all over, taste her until he got enough…which wouldn't be any time soon. She had become an itch he needed to scratch—but way below the surface. The stark reality of just how much he wanted her loomed in the back of his mind, but he couldn't deal with that now. For him to desire any woman to this degree was unheard of, totally crazy. Insane. And he simply refused to admit to the possibility that he, the master of seduction, was the one getting seduced.

And with that possibility flashing through his mind

like a bold warning, he suddenly freed her mouth to draw back to look at her, observe her in silence. Her eyes were closed, she was breathing heavily and her lips looked liked they'd been thoroughly kissed. But the main thought in his mind, what he considered as a major accomplishment, was that she was in his bed, flat on her back beneath him.

He knew at that moment that she was fully aware, just like he was, of what could or would happen next. Here, in this bed with her, a bed he'd never shared with another woman, the thought of which had fueled his lust since meeting her.

She slowly opened her eyes and looked up at him. He looked back and what he saw was a beautiful woman whose hair was tumbled around a flushed face, and whose honey-brown eyes had a degree of warmth that symbolized a level of passion he rarely saw in a woman.

Enthralled, he held her gaze, wanting more than anything to get naked and sink into the deep, luscious depths of her. On his tongue he tasted her, even while imagining another taste of her he wanted to become familiar with. Her intimate taste. The thought of doing so made his sex surge, and he knew she felt it when it did.

"You're trying to seduce me," she whispered as fragments of passion exploded bit by bit, inch by inch in his stomach from the sound of her voice. He was getting turned on even more seeing her lips move.

There was only one response he could give her, one of complete honesty. "Yes, I am trying to seduce you." And then helpless to do or say anything else at that moment, he lowered his head to kiss her again.

Chapter 9

This, Natalie thought, was a deliberate seduction, as calculated as it could get. And just as shrewd. Vastly intimate. There was no doubt in her mind that he was a master at it, had years of experience and had sharpened his skills just for her.

His tongue was having a field day with hers, driving her to the brink of madness by bringing forth ideas in her mind that she'd never considered before. A part of her desperately wanted to believe that his kissing her this way was a waste of his time, that she was immune to such seductive tactics. But another part of her, the one that was enjoying the feel of his tongue mating with hers, wasn't sure just how strong her willpower was.

Over the years she had encountered a number of men who'd wanted to take her to bed to not only dissect her mind but to break it down in the process. They'd felt threatened by her intellect, and when she refused to let their ruse work, they began feeling intimidated and saw her as a bother. She had handled their rebuff by displaying her competency even more. As far as she was concerned, not wanting to accept her as an equal was their problem and not hers. As a result, she'd been labeled problematic. That, coupled with her desire not to ever encounter a man close to Karl in attitude and temperament, had forced her long ago to take herself out of the game. That was one of the reasons she thought Donovan Steele was as lethal as they came.

There was nothing typical with him. Everything seemed out of the ordinary. She was way out of her league with him, beyond her limited experience with men.

Through the heat consuming her with their kiss, she was instantly aware of him lifting her tank top and knew she should resist him. Instead she moaned deep in her throat when she felt a tingling sensation flood her belly beneath the warmth of the hand he placed on her stomach. Moments later, his hand moved, shifting upward and unfastening the front clasp of her bra. And then, without missing a beat, his mouth followed to her breast.

That's when she lost touch with reality and lost her grip on any control she had. His tongue stroked her nipples and she became engrossed, totally, irrefutably absorbed in the sensations ripping through her. He was devouring her breasts with the same greed he had bestowed on her lips. Each suck and lick to her nipples elicited a deep pull in the area between her legs. She suddenly felt sensitive there as sensations deluged her. And at that moment she felt the need to whisper his name.

"Donovan."

Donovan was fully aware of the moment Natalie said his name, and the passionate tone had his erection throbbing. He wanted to hear her say it again, but right on the verge of having an orgasm. Her scent was hot and enticing, and was getting to him in the most primitive way.

He moved his hand to the elastic waistband of her shorts and without giving himself much time to think about what he was doing, he eased his hand inside and quickly moved past the silky panties she was wearing, going straight to her feminine mound.

The moment he touched her there, his fingers making contact with her wetness, he heard her release a litany of deep moans. The sound, as well as her intimate response to the area he was touching, drove him over the edge. His desire to taste her became overwhelming. Elemental.

Giving a final thorough lick to her breasts, he quickly went into action by pulling her shorts and panties down her legs. Before she could deny him access, he lowered his head between her thighs, and his mouth went straight to the heated folds of her femininity.

On instinct her hips thrust upward, and he grabbed her hips to hold her there, needing to devour her with a hunger that focused his senses on this particular part of her body. With practiced licks and precise flicks of his tongue, he tasted the invigorating sweetness of her blazing fire, her steamy passion, and he didn't plan to let up any time soon—not until he made her come.

That didn't take long. When her thighs began trembling, he knew she was about ready to detonate. Every nerve and muscle in his body was poised, prepared and primed for the experience. And when it happened and she screamed out his name, he continued the intimate kiss, claiming this part of her as his. Intense pride filled his chest at the sounds of pleasure she was making. He held nothing back and neither did she. The next time, he silently vowed, he wanted to be staring her in the eyes when it happened. And there *would* be a next time.

He continued kissing her while at the same time giving her body time to recover. It was only then that he withdrew his mouth, eased back up her panties and shorts before sliding up her body to look at her. Her eyes had a glazed look, and she seemed momentarily at a loss for words.

She moved her mouth as if she was going to say something, and he quickly decided that he wasn't ready for her to say anything. So he leaned closer, bent his head. Her lips parted and he slid in his tongue and kissed her, sharing her own taste with her. Moments later he reluctantly pulled his mouth away.

She looked up at him. "That should not have happened, Donovan."

He figured she would say something like that. "But it did. You and I both wanted it to happen. We enjoyed it. Admit it," he countered.

Natalie wasn't ready to admit anything. Her mind

had practically turned to mush, and she couldn't even think straight. She'd arrived this morning to clean his house, not to be the recipient of mouth sex. And especially not to the point at which it had made her scream. She was the most disciplined person she knew, and she had screamed.

"Admit it, Natalie."

She narrowed her gaze and wished she could ignore what had happened between them. Ignore him and that smile curving his lips. So she glanced around the room and said, "I need to finish up in here and leave."

The smile curving his lips widened. "So that's the way you want to play?"

She had news for him; she hadn't wanted to play at all and had been doing just fine remaining on the sidelines. He and his naughty tongue had definitely thrown a monkey wrench into things. The vivid memory of his head between her legs had her blushing.

"Like I said, today was a mistake," she reemphasized.

Donovan quirked a dark brow and recognized her ploy for what it was. She still wasn't ready to acknowledge what was between them, what he wasn't about to let slide by. She had said she thought today was a mistake, but she hadn't said it wouldn't happen again. Evidently she had missed that fact and he was glad.

Deciding he had pushed her buttons enough for one day, he eased into a sitting position. He glanced around the room when she got up off the bed. "There's nothing else you need to do in here," he said.

He noted she tried looking everywhere but at him when she said, "There's plenty I need to do. I haven't dusted, vacuumed the floor or changed the linen," she said briskly.

"Don't worry about dusting or vacuuming in here today. And I don't want my linen changed, Natalie. Your scent is absorbed into the sheets, and I want it to stay that way for a while."

She tilted her head and met his gaze. The air suddenly became charged again. Intimate. Sexually explosive. She moistened her lips with the tip of her tongue before replying, "Suit yourself."

He gave her a slight smile. "I did and I'm extremely satisfied."

She began backing up toward the door. "Well, if you're sure you don't want me to do anything else in here, then I'll be going."

"I'm sure."

"And I'll be contacting you sometime next week to discuss my replacement," she added firmly.

"No, you won't. There will be no replacement, Natalie."

Her eyes widened and then glared. "Surely you don't think that I can continue to be your housekeeper after what happened here today."

"I'm afraid that's exactly what I think. It's what I know."

He knew his words sounded arrogant, more than a little presumptuous and selfishly cocky. He watched her body stiffen and would not have been surprised if she had thrown some object off his dresser at him. Instead, after glaring at him for a second, she moved closer to his bedroom door.

"If you get restless and edgy later, just come back.

I'll be here. And if not tonight, I'm available any night. If I'm not here just let yourself in." Donovan heard himself give the invite, and a part of him couldn't believe he'd actually done so.

Instead of answering him, she rushed out of the bedroom and hurried down the stairs.

Just as well, he thought, easing off the bed. Other than his cousins and sisters-in-law, no other woman had ever been given unlimited access to his home. It was evident that he had it bad for Natalie. But he inwardly assured himself he could handle this temporary bout of madness and that the only reason he was being so indulging with her, so abnormally reckless, was because they had only five weeks left to be together. He was confident by the time her aunt was back on her feet and had resumed her position as his housekeeper that he would have worked Natalie out of his system.

The sound of the front door opening and closing signaled that she was gone.

"How did things go today, Nat?"

Natalie glanced over at Aunt Earline as they sat together at the dinner table. The question was one her aunt asked every day, and Natalie thought that if she was truthful and told her just how things went today, Earline Darwin would be mortified. Aunt Earline must never know that although she and Donovan hadn't gone all the way, she had been in his bed and together they had practically made kissing an art form, and that in the end he had lapped her up pretty good. Right into an orgasm. Even now her inner thighs felt extremely warm, and she had to hold her legs together real tight just thinking about what Donovan had done between them.

She plastered a smile on her face. "Everything was okay." There. She'd given a short answer. That was that.

Apparently not when Aunt Earline further asked. "So this change in days works for Donovan Steele?"

She couldn't help recalling how he'd been conveniently home when she had gotten there and the somewhat smug look on his face when she'd left. "Yes, apparently it does. I was in and out of there in no time." *But not before he got me on my back and did some scandalous things to my body.*

"That's good."

Yes, she inwardly admitted, although she didn't want to do so. It had been good. Too good. The inner workings of her body were now clamoring for a repeat performance. The unshakable Dr. Natalie Ford had been shaken to the core.

An hour or so later she was pacing around the house like a caged bird that needed its freedom. She and Farrah had planned to go out again tonight, somewhere other than the Racetrack Café, but Farrah had canceled their plans because she had to work late.

It was early but Aunt Earline had already retired for the night. She planned to watch her all-time favorite movie, *Dirty Dancing,* for the umpteenth time before going to sleep. Her aunt had encouraged her to go out and have some fun tonight, with or without Farrah.

As she paced, she couldn't get Donovan's invitation out of her mind. "If you get restless and edgy later, just come back. I'll be here."

The man definitely had some arrogant nerves in his body. What woman would even think about taking him up on his offer? Natalie dropped her face in the palms of her hands and ashamedly admitted that *she* was.

She slumped down on the sofa. Should she really be ashamed? What was wrong if she did consider having a fling with him? At least she knew where he stood. She definitely wasn't looking for love and neither was he. In fact if she was thinking about a fling then he would be the perfect candidate. He was probably an expert at flings.

In addition to that, she didn't have to worry about him getting all crazy on her if he somehow found out she was a chemistry professor at an Ivy League university instead of a bona fide cleaning woman, not if the relationship was sexual and nothing more. And when it was over—for however long it lasted, which would be no more than five more weeks at best—she would return to Princeton, New Jersey, feeling renewed and energized. Farrah had been right Friday night. A meaningless fling with Donovan would give her a new attitude.

She was twenty-six, a professional, a woman who deserved to indulge in a fling or two. She had realized a long time ago that it would be close to difficult to find a man willing to come into her world, and most of the male counterparts she'd found were too stuffy and boring. None had ever come close to attracting her attention the way Donovan had. Besides, he could be the one to prove whether or not Karl's verdict on her skill as a bed partner was true. A part of her always wondered. Donovan had proved Karl wrong with the kissing, and she couldn't help wonder if he would prove the other part false, as well.

Natalie eased to her feet. There was only one way to find out.

Donovan tightened his grip on the telephone in his hand. "Okay, Morgan, thanks for keeping me in the loop. We figured sooner or later word of what we were doing would leak out," he said. "We're good as long as the trade secrets don't get into the wrong hands."

"You're right," Morgan said. "But I'll feel a lot better when that Product Trade Show is over."

Donovan talked to Morgan a few minutes longer before hanging up the phone. For any business, the exploitation of trade secrets was a serious matter and the protection of them was complicated at best, especially when chemical formulas were involved. One of their competitors had again tried obtaining information, which meant SC was determined more than ever to make sure that didn't happen.

He glanced at his watch and saw it was close to eight. He had thought about going over to the Racetrack Café for a while to hang out with Bronson and the guys, but for some reason he wasn't in the mood. What he was in the mood for was sex. Even now, his manhood was twitching for release of the most elemental and primitive kind. He had a list of women who were amenable to a booty call tonight, but he only wanted one particular woman. Natalie.

He sucked in a deep, satisfying breath when he recalled how earlier that day he had gone down on her, but not before feasting on her breasts. Every muscle and every fiber in his body had been attuned to her.

He then pulled in a frustrated breath at the thought that what he'd done today might have scared her away. He didn't want to think about the possibility that he had pushed her to the limit, and she would make good on her threat to send in a replacement, or better yet, convince her aunt to drop him as a client.

With nothing better to do, he was about to head back to his office to finish reading the Gleeve-Ware report he'd started on earlier when there was a knock at his door. Thinking it was probably Bronson, Myles or Uri dropping by, he crossed the room in his bare feet and opened the door. His jaw almost dropped.

Standing at his door was Natalie, and she was wearing a black miniskirt and a low-cut white blouse that clearly showed she wasn't wearing a bra. Not that she needed one with her full and round breasts.

He took in her outfit and how gorgeous her legs looked in it before returning his gaze back to her face. He stared at her while his manhood, which had been twitching earlier, broke out into a full-fledged throb.

She stared back before saying in what he thought was a soft, ultra sexy voice, "You said to come back if I got to feeling restless and edgy." She took a minute to breathe in before adding. "And I'm here."

Chapter 10

Everything happened in such rapid succession that Natalie wasn't sure who made the first move. The thing she did remember was Donovan reaching out and pulling her inside and slamming the door shut behind her. After that she recalled the moment he lowered his mouth to hers, which resulted in a heated exchange of lips and tongues. And she did remember the moment he swept her into his arms to carry her up the stairs, not breaking the kiss in the process.

But what was kind of fuzzy was what brought on what was happening now. He had stopped halfway up the stairs and lowered her bottom to the step to lift up her skirt where he then proceeded to rip off her drenched panties.

"I need one quick taste," he said huskily and with an

intensity that she felt all the way to her toes. And before she could blink, he had knelt between her legs and lowered his head to penetrate her deeply with his tongue.

She fought for control, but the only thing she could do was grab the wood railing, totally helpless against the myriad of sensations that shot through her as he used his tongue to stroke her wetter. She was on the verge of exploding when he suddenly withdrew his mouth and stood up, towering over her.

"Can't wait to make it upstairs," he said, lowering his zipper and then quickly removing his jeans and briefs. He held on to his jeans long enough to pull out a condom packet that he ripped opened with his teeth. Then he tossed the jeans away.

Through passion-glazed eyes, she watched as he put the condom on his engorged shaft. She'd never seen Karl perform such a task, and watching Donovan prepare himself inflamed her senses. He was big, a lot bigger than Karl, which had her wondering if perhaps she should be worried.

She quickly dismissed the notion from her mind when he dropped back down to his knees in front of her. He then reached out and grabbed hold of her hips in a firm grip, lifting her bottom off the step while inching his body toward hers, opening her legs wider in the process.

A quiver of anticipation raced through every part of her body. When he leaned closer and began easing his shaft inside of her, holding her gaze while doing so, for one unguarded moment she allowed herself to let go.

Donovan, however struggled for control. It took

everything within him not to thrust hard in the wake of the excruciating pleasure being inside of her brought. Never would he have thought that passing through territory he had never been in before would give him such exquisite pleasure. Her body was tight but was stretching to accommodate his size. And his hands continued to hold tight to her hips while tilting up her bottom for a more perfect fit.

A soft whimper, which he hoped was the result of intense pleasure, escaped from between her lips when he finally reached the hilt. Then she threw her head back and released an intense feminine groan. The sound was electrifying and sent shivers down his spine, propelling him to move within her.

He began riding her slowly at first, absorbing her scent through his nostrils and fighting to retain control while waves of intense pleasure washed over him with pulsating intensity.

Adrenaline rushed forward, gushed through his veins and swelled his erection inside her even more. He heard her breath catch at the same moment her inner muscles clamped down on him. They tightened, holding his shaft hostage, and he nearly lost control. He regained it and began moving within her again with a possessiveness he'd never demonstrated toward any other woman.

He lifted her hips higher off the step, not allowing his hold to ease even the slightest bit while establishing a rhythm that taunted her and challenged him. He heard her moans, and they threatened to drive him over the edge as he thrusted back and forth inside of her with lightning speed. And she was meeting his thrusts, stroke for stroke. They were making love on the stairs of all places, but the place didn't matter—only the outcome.

And the outcome was more than he'd bargained for. He released a guttural moan just seconds before she screamed his name as she was plunged into a state of ecstasy. Her orgasm ignited bursts of pleasure within him at the same time his body shattered in a huge explosion of its own. She clung to him and wrapped her feet securely around his back. Desire sank deep into his pores, and he felt himself being thrown into some unknown abyss.

He bent his head to capture her lips. Refusing to leave her body, he kept a firm grip on her hips as sensations rammed through him nonstop until his release left him feeling drained but completely satisfied. He knew he was in deep trouble when, moments later, he started getting hard again.

This time he wanted to make love to her in a bed. His bed. He withdrew from her body, gathered her into his arms and carried her the rest of the way up the stairs.

Natalie wondered if she would ever be able to move again. She seriously doubted it. After making love with Donovan—on of all places—the stairs, he had brought her up to his bedroom where he finished undressing her and had made love to her all over again. He made love as intensely and thoroughly as he probably did everything else, and more than once he had whispered in a deep, husky voice just how much he enjoyed it. She believed he had, which meant Karl had said all those things only to hurt her.

"You're awake from your nap," that same deep, husky voice said now.

She found the strength to glance over at Donovan. He was lying beside her, one of his legs was thrown over hers as if holding her captive. She couldn't miss the fact that they were both naked. After making love with him, she had drifted off to sleep, too exhausted to keep her eyes open any longer. To most people dozing at this hour would equate to retiring for the night, but since she intended to sleep in her bed at her aunt's house, Donovan was right: she had only taken a nap. A much needed one. But now she was wide awake.

She glanced over at the clock on his nightstand. "It's late. I need go."

"Not yet. We need to talk."

Tension settled in the back of her neck. She had a feeling she knew what he wanted to talk about. Given his reputation, she was surprised they hadn't had the discussion before he'd taken her on the stairs. "I already know what you want to say," she said.

"Do you?"

"Yes. You don't want me to assume what we've done means anything of substance and that you aren't the marrying kind and prefer short, meaningless affairs."

He stared at her and didn't say anything for a moment. Then he asked, "Knowing all of that, where does it leave you?"

She couldn't help but smile. Lord help him, but the man actually thought every woman would be forever scarred because of his rejection. "That leaves me with what I want most, too."

"Which is?"

"A good life without any man cluttering it up."

His brow rose before he responded. "I recall you saying you'd taken a break from men."

"It's more than a break, actually," she said, widening her smile. "I'm no more interested in a serious involvement with a man than you are with a woman, so you can lower your guard and sleep peacefully tonight."

He would, Donovan thought, although for some reason it bothered him that she could so easily wipe him off. Why did she have to be so accepting of his stance on affairs? Why did he feel so annoyed by hers?

She made a move to get up, but his leg hindered her progress. She frowned. "Do you mind?"

Yes, he did mind—about a number of things that he really wasn't even sure about. One thing was for certain, though. He didn't like how easy it was for her to dust off what they'd just shared. Maybe he should be relieved that she wasn't the clingy type, that she was mature enough to engage in a meaningless affair and know how to move on. That she wouldn't be entertaining any lingering side effects from it. But still. He had made her scream—several times. He'd given her multiple orgasms. Her leg print was probably a permanent imprint in his back. He had been inside her so much tonight that his shaft would probably be suffering from withdrawals starting tomorrow. He was beginning to get awfully pissed that the one woman who affected him like none other was acting as if he hadn't made an impression on her at all, lasting or otherwise.

"Donovan?"

He met her gaze deciding she had underestimated a Steele. "Yes?"

"Would you move your leg?"

"I don't think so." Instead of moving his leg, he shifted his body to straddle her.

Her gaze narrowed up at him. "And just what do you think you're doing?"

"About to get some more of you."

"And if I don't want to give you more?"

An arrogant smile touched the corners of his lips. "Then it's up to me to convince you that you really do. Seduction is my specialty." He leaned down and captured her mouth with his.

Just that quick desire spiked up his spine. When she begin kissing him back with a need just as ravenous as his, he knew he had her convinced. But that wasn't enough. Not by a long shot. He wanted to hear her scream some more.

Moments later he broke their kiss only to trail his mouth down the base of her neck toward her chest and greedily latched onto a breast. Both were pretty, shaped with perfection, appealing to any man's eyes, definitely a tasty treat to his tongue. As he worked that tongue to her breasts, taking the nipples in his mouth, sucking for a while and then using his tongue to give unadulterated pleasure, her moans began coming and the sound taunted his control. He knew women well enough to know she was almost over the edge, and he wouldn't be happy until he was tumbling off the cliff with her.

Feeling a heady rush of pleasure at the sensuous state he now had her in, he moved away from her breasts to trek further south when, in one heck of a surprising move and totally catching him off guard, she slid from beneath him and with a shove to his chest sent him tumbling on his back. He blinked to find she was now the one straddling him.

"Are you ready to be punished, Donovan?" she asked.

He swallowed deeply. "Depends on how you plan to dish it out." The look in her eyes warned him that whatever she had in mind would probably be brutal and that he was in for a lot of suffering.

"So, you want some more of me, huh?"

He couldn't tell a lie although admitting such a thing could be tantamount to acknowledging something he'd rather keep to himself. He was becoming addicted to her. "As much of you as I can get and then some," he said, actually with little regret.

"And you think you can handle whatever I give you?" she asked as her hand skittered over his chest. His reaction to her touch was instantaneous, and he watched a haughty smile touch her lips when his shaft got even more engorged. Before he could answer, she swept her hand downward and captured him in a firm, yet painless, grip.

He suppressed the urge to groan, but that didn't stop the shiver of arousal that shot through his body knowing she held him in her hand. He barely got the words out in a strained voice. "Yes, I can handle it," he said, when in fact he wasn't so sure.

"Um, I hope for your sake that you can." And then in a quick and surprising move, she lowered her head and went down on him.

Chapter 11

There was no way she was going to let him know she was a novice at this, Natalie thought, using her mouth in a way she'd only heard about and hoping she was doing it right. Apparently she was, if the way his fingers were clutching her hair was anything to go by.

And then there was the way he was breathing—ragged, choppy and at times uneven while making a number of groaning sounds. She tried to ignore all of that while her tongue did all the things to him she would secretly admit to fantasizing about in her nightly dreams. She had never considered doing this to Karl or any man, but with Donovan there was something about his scent that enticed her to sample his taste.

"I can't take any more," he said in a jagged breath

while at the same time clenching her shoulders in an attempt to pry her enthusiastic mouth from him. He pulled her up over his body, and lifting his head from the pillow he met her mouth, taking it with a greedy intent and a voracious hunger.

Supported by an arm on both sides of him, Natalie let him plunder her mouth at an insatiable will, returning the kiss with the same fervor that he was delivering, not believing that after all they'd done already that night they still were going strong with no thoughts of letting up. At least she wasn't, and by the way he was avidly feeding on her mouth, neither was he.

But she wasn't through with him yet. She was determined to make her brand of torture bittersweet. Ignoring his protest, she pulled away from the heated kiss and licked her lips before saying. "You weren't supposed to do that."

He flashed a wicked grin that held no remorse. "Sorry about that."

"I'm accepting no apologies. You're going to pay."

The look he gave her was one of incredulity. "With more torture?"

She smiled sweetly. "I'll let you decide. Now hand me a condom, please."

Shifting slightly, he reached over into the nightstand and pulled out a condom packet and ripped it open with his teeth. He handed the condom to her before tossing the opened foil packet to join the others littering the floor.

"Look at the mess you've made," she said, grinning. "I'm sure your housekeeper thinks you're a slob."

Donovan couldn't help but chuckle. "Then I'm

going to have to convince her otherwise," he said, trying to retain his composure as he watched her sheath his erection and noted how fascinated she seemed with the entire process. That wouldn't be so bad if the hands touching his shaft weren't so warm. They reminded him of the warmth of her mouth on him.

"There." Finished with the task, she then eased her body in place over his and centered her feminine mound right over the head of his engorged member.

"That's right, sweetheart, take me on home," he said in a tormented breath. "Lead me right inside of you."

"Um, what if I say that I don't want to?"

He arched a brow. "Then I would say you've got to be kidding."

She couldn't help but smile at that. "No, I'm not kidding," she said, while deliberating easing the lower part of her body down a little so that her feminine mound could lightly brush against his shaft. He sucked in a deep breath at the fleeting contact.

"What's the matter, Donovan? Can't you handle it? Can't you handle me?"

For the first time in his life, Donovan actually wondered if perhaps there was a woman he couldn't handle, and he was flat on his back staring up at her. The thought of that was absurd, ludicrous at best. But then, he was the one who seemed to be suffering, and she appeared to be having the time of her life increasing his misery.

Donovan inwardly sighed. His mama always told him you could catch more flies with honey than with vinegar, and he was willing to put it to the test. He reached out and wrapped his arms around her neck. "Are you sure you want to keep agonizing me?" he asked, lifting his head up to lick the corners of her mouth with his tongue. He then used that same tongue to trace the outline of her lips and watched the simmering fire he was igniting in her gaze.

He took a breast into his hand, fondled the nipple with his fingertips. He sensed the moment when passion instead of punishment took over her mind. Now it was time to put the icing on the cake by seducing her with words of what he wanted to do to her and how he intended to do it. He spoke deliberately low but made sure he could be heard as well as understood. He was explicit, described everything in detail, every single position, giving her an unscripted idea of just what his plans were for her. His words were breaking through. He could tell by the darkening of her eyes and the unsteady sound of her breathing. He could also tell by her feminine scent. His words had lubricated her even more.

She tipped her head back and stared at him, and he wondered if she realized that her lower body had inched down a little, and that the blunt head of his shaft had penetrated her somewhat. It was inching forward, stretching her again to make the intimate connection possible.

He continued talking, making promises, while their bodies connected. But that didn't stop him from cupping her backside in his hand to hold her in place, or locking his leg around her just in case she had a change of heart. Their bodies were now locked, and he didn't intend on letting her go anywhere. With that thought in his mind, he lifted his hips off the bed to fill her even more.

Now it was time to deliver on all those promises he'd made.

Before she had time to react, he thrust in hard, almost retreated and then thrust in hard again. In response she moved her body to the rhythm he'd set, riding him as hard as he needed to be ridden. Never had he made love to a woman with so much intensity, an all-out assault on delivering passion to her on a silver platter. The same way she was delivering it to him.

Somehow with their vigorous entanglements they had changed positions, and he was now the one on top. He tilted her hips at an angle to drive relentlessly into her. He was never into drama, but as far as he was concerned, you couldn't get any more dramatic than this. This was lovemaking at its finest, the kind that made multiple orgasms commonplace. She was bringing something out of him that he'd not known had been inside of him.

"Donovan!"

No matter how many times he heard her scream his name, it always did something to him. It triggered his engorged sex locked inside of her to react. To explode in one hell of a release. She grabbed hold of his shoulders. Her nails dug deep into his shoulder blades, but pain wasn't the dominant factor right now. The passionate flames burning through his veins were. And even as he felt her come apart in his arms and he exploded in an orgasm that had rocked him to the core, he couldn't stop thrusting into her, needing this. Needing her.

He quickly pushed away the thought that he would need any woman, no matter how enjoyable the lovemaking was. Tomorrow he would deal with all these foreign emotions swamping him now. But not tonight. Tonight he wanted only to deal with this. Immeasurable pleasure.

Natalie glanced at the clock as she eased out of bed from under Donovan's arms. She was glad her aunt was a sound sleeper and probably didn't know that it was close to five in the morning and she hadn't returned home yet.

She glanced around for her clothes and then quickly remembered Donovan had stripped her naked on the stairs. The memories had sensuous shivers moving up her spine. The man had more passion in his little toe than Karl had had in his entire body. Donovan may be a tad arrogant, but the man could certainly deliver. He had made good on all those promises he had whispered and had introduced her to lovemaking positions she hadn't known existed. Her body was sore but she felt good. She couldn't even count the number of orgasms she'd had tonight. To say she had made up for lost time was an understatement.

She wrapped her arms around her naked body as she glanced over at Donovan sleeping peacefully in the bed he'd found her in that day. Leaning back over to the bed, she brushed a kiss first on his cheek and then his lips, being careful not to wake him.

One and done.

At least she knew where she stood with Donovan. He had spelled out his expectations—or lack of them—loud and clear. One night of extreme pleasure and it was done, never to be repeated. A one-night stand, nothing more, nothing less. He had definitely gotten rid of her restlessness and had taken the edge off. She would always have memories of their night together.

Backing away from the bed, she turned to slip out the door but not before glancing back over her shoulder at him. Whether she wanted him to or not, Donovan had a special place in her heart.

Donovan nearly jumped straight up out of bed at the ringing of the phone. With hazy eyes, he glanced around the room trying to recall what day it was. Then he remembered. It was Saturday morning.

He leaned over and snatched the phone out of its cradle. "Hello?"

"Hey, we thought we'd get together and have break-fast at your place before heading over to the gym," his brother Morgan said in the phone. "I'll make a pit stop at Mary's Diner. You want the usual?"

Donovan raked a hand down his face in an attempt to wipe the sleep from his eyes. "Yes, the usual will be fine." Then his stomach growled, and he remem-bered the intense sexual activities from the night before. "Make it a double order for me, though."

He hung up the phone and slumped back down in bed. Jeeze. What a night. If there was such a thing as having a sexual hangover then this was it. He shifted his body to look down at the floor. There were condom packets everywhere. Damn. How many of the blasted things had he used? If he thought all that action last night was a result of a dream, then he was looking at viable proof that it wasn't. And just when had Natalie left? How could he have slept through her slipping out of bed? She at least deserved a walk to the car.

Knowing he needed to get up since his brothers were on their way over, he eased out of bed and headed toward the bathroom. And he needed to get rid of any evidence of his activities of the night before or his brothers would never let him live it down. He chuckled thinking that they actually thought they could share such things with a wife. Not that he thought any of his sisters-in-laws were prudes by any means, but still. Some of the positions he had introduced Natalie to last night were scandalous at best. But she seemed to have enjoyed them as much as he had.

A half hour later he had showered, dressed, discarded all those used condom packets off his bedroom floor and picked up his clothes that had been scattered all over the staircase.

By the time his brothers arrived, he figured he looked like a man well-rested with no signs of what had happened the night before. Apparently not. Bas walked in, took one look at him and said, "Damn, Donovan, what's with all those passion marks on your neck? Rough night, huh, kid? No wonder you wanted a double order."

Donovan rolled his eyes. Leave it to Bas to notice such things. Now of course Chance and Morgan were now giving him their full attention. "Don't worry about any marks on my neck," he growled, taking the breakfast bag from Bas's hands.

Still, he couldn't help walking over to the mirror on his foyer wall to take a look for himself. Bas was right. He did have passion marks all over his neck. Usually he was the giver of such things, never the recipient.

"Evidently you had a wild one on your hands last night," Bas said, laughing, clearly amused.

Normally, any jokes his brothers made about his conquests wouldn't bother him in the least, but since his bed partner had been Natalie, for some reason it did bother him. Yes, she had been wild but he had driven her to it. He had been relentless to see how often he could make her come. "I'd rather not discuss it," he said to the three and saw the surprised look in their gazes.

"Okay." Chance nodded. "If that's how it is."

In all honesty, Donovan wasn't sure just how it was, but until he sorted everything out in his head, he merely said, "Yes, that's how it is." And then he tacked on something he figured he would never, ever say about a woman. "She's different."

Farrah raised a brow as she gazed across the table at Natalie. "That's the fourth time you've yawned in fifteen minutes. Didn't you get any sleep last night?"

Natalie couldn't help but shift in her seat under her friend's intense stare. And she was sure she was blushing. Instead of answering, she tried changing the subject. "Do you remember Gail Porter, that girl who used to sit in the back of the class and not talk to anyone, until that day she got up in front of the class to do her report and told us her parents had taken her to a nudist camp? I wonder what happened to her."

Farrah simply smiled over the top of her menu. "I understand she moved away, got married and now has some top-level job at the White House."

A surprised expression touched Natalie's features. "Really?" she asked, incredulously.

With a straight face, Farrah simply answered, "No."

Natalie narrowed her eyes. "That was mean."

Farrah laughed out loud. "What's mean is you not answering my question about your lack of sleep last night. Now are you ready to tell me where you went last night?"

No, she wasn't. Instead, Natalie took a sip of her water. Luckily, her aunt had been asleep when she had returned home this morning just moments before the delivery boy had thrown the paper in the yard. Without taking a shower, she had crawled between the sheets with the scent of Donovan still clinging to her skin and memories of their lovemaking in her mind.

"Natalie?"

Knowing Farrah wouldn't let up until she was given an answer, she looked across the table, met her inquisitive gaze and said, "I was with Donovan."

Farrah lifted a brow. "And?"

"And what?"

Farrah rolled her eyes. "What do you mean you were with him? Did the two of you meet up at the Racetrack Café? Did you go out on a date someplace else? Did you—"

"I was at his house. I spent the night."

The corners of Farrah's lips curled up in a smile. "By spending the night do you mean you slept in a guest room? Did the two of you sit on the sofa all night watching movies and holding hands? Did the—"

"We slept together," an annoyed Natalie leaned over and whispered curtly. Farrah liked getting details. "But we didn't get much sleep for mating like rabbits all night long." She narrowed her gaze and snapped, "Satisfied?"

A smirk of a grin appeared on Farrah's face. "Forget about me. Are *you* satisfied?"

Natalie blinked, not expecting Farrah's retort. Natalie leaned back in her chair. Relaxed. Settled. Not as sore as she had been that morning. She couldn't help but smile. "Yes, I'm satisfied. Extremely. Exceedingly. Enormously. Tre—"

"Cut! I got the picture."

Natalie knew that Farrah really didn't. There was no way anyone could get the picture of what had gone on inside Donovan's bedroom last night, and in a way that was a good thing. The picture would have been erotic, X-rated at best.

"So he was worth all those years of holding out?" Farrah asked.

She nodded. "Every single moment I spent with my head in a book, working on projects and trying hard to forget men existed. Yes, he was worth it."

Farrah smiled. "Then I'm happy you got the experience. When will you see him again?"

Natalie shook her head. "I might see him again but not that way. What we shared last night was a fling— a one-night fling. It won't be repeated. That's what we both agreed."

Farrah didn't say anything for a moment and then said. "That might be easier said than done, Nat."

Natalie was glad the waitress appeared at that

moment to take their order or she would have been forced to admit Farrah was right.

Donovan pulled his damp T-shirt over his head and tossed it in the dirty-clothes hamper. Today the basketball game between him and his brothers had been brutal. Evidently there had been a lot of frustrations to unleash. Still, he felt good. Not that he'd had to work off much masculine energy since he'd done so last night.

He left the laundry room and walked into the kitchen where he immediately headed for the refrigerator and opened it up. He pulled the beer from the six-pack Uri had left a few weeks ago, popped the tab and then took a long pleasurable gulp.

A satisfied smile touched his moist lips, which he wiped with the back of his hand. Life couldn't be better. Then he glanced around the kitchen and thought that life couldn't be lonelier.

He frowned, wondering where in the hell that thought had come from. A lonely Steele? How could that be when he had brothers and cousins living in the same city? And he could always catch a flight to Phoenix, Chicago, Miami or Boston and visit his relatives there.

He went over to the window and glanced out. What would it be like to come home to a house he shared with someone? Not just someone, but the woman with whom he'd spent the night in bed. Could he even imagine building a life with one woman, building a family and having children, building his own dynasty like his brothers were doing?

It didn't take a rocket scientist to see they were happy, had eased into the roles of husbands and family men without a hitch. He'd always figured he was different, didn't want the things they did and totally enjoyed his freedom. So why was he even considering otherwise?

He took another gulp of beer, emptying the can. Moving away from the window, he placed the empty can on the counter. He'd promised Bron and the guys that he would drop by the café tonight since he hadn't shown up last night, as was the norm. But he had no regrets. Last night he was here in bed with a woman that still had his heart pounding each time he thought about how his body had plummeted into multiple orgasms while inside of her.

Natalie had shown him, proven beyond a shadow of a doubt that no two women were the same. He had met his match, and even after making love to her last night, he wanted her again.

Chapter 12

Natalie sat at the desk in her aunt's office as she worked on the schedules for next week. It had been a week since she had made love to Donovan in his huge bed. She hadn't heard from him, but she hadn't really expected any contact. Like she had told Farrah, she and Donovan fully understood each other. He didn't want anything beyond what they'd shared Friday night and neither did she.

She'd been keeping herself pretty busy. The agency had taken on three new employees, and she'd been busy working them into the schedule. Her aunt's doctor visit this week indicated she was healing nicely, and Natalie was happy for that. So it was her opinion that life was good.

But that didn't mean she didn't have those dreams

each night in which Donovan had a starring role. And now that she knew how it felt to make love with a man who was just as giving as he was taking, she knew he had tilted the scales and she doubted another man would ever affect her the way he had. She'd been dealing with elements of chemistry since she'd won her first science fair in the eighth grade, but Donovan had the ability to ignite a totally different kind of chemistry, the type she wasn't accustomed to dealing with. And then there were those funny little feelings that would start fluttering around her heart whenever she thought of him. They were feelings that could grow into something more than she wanted them to be. They were feelings that had more to do with the human anatomy than with chemistry.

She'd gone to pull one of the client's records from the file cabinet when her cell phone rang. She quickly picked it up. "Yes?"

"Dr. Ford, this is Dr. Stanley."

Natalie lifted her brow in surprise. Dr. Miriam Stanley headed the global study of the troposphere for NASA, and they had worked closely on various projects over the past two years. "Dr. Stanley, this is a pleasant surprise. Is anything wrong?"

"No, everything is fine. However, I was hoping I could request your assistance on short notice."

"In what way?" Natalie asked, leaning back on the desk. She was already reviewing formulas for NASA that could imply a continental pollution source for industrial emissions.

"We will be hosting a number of government officials on the Princeton campus next Friday, and we were wondering if you could be included on a panel for a discussion on global warming."

Next Friday? Natalie nibbled on her bottom lip trying to determine if it could work. Her aunt was doing fine so flying back to Princeton for a couple of days wouldn't be so bad. She could fly out Thursday night and fly back Saturday morning. "Yes, I'd love to participate."

"Thank you. I'll e-mail you a number of the key discussion topics," Dr. Stanley said.

A few minutes later Natalie hung up the phone, still smiling. She knew her name had been tossed about as a possible person who could sit on the Global Warming Commission. To do so would be an outstanding accomplishment. She needed to start jotting down the key points she intended to discuss, and hopefully, doing so would keep her mind occupied for a while.

Donovan released a deep breath when he heard the sound of the front door opening. That meant Natalie had arrived for the weekly cleaning of his home. And again he'd taken a work-at-home day. He hated admitting that he'd been looking forward to this day all week long—and had even contemplated calling her during the week. But then he would remember their agreement. What they'd shared had been a one-night stand and nothing more.

Still, he couldn't discount the fact that she had been on his mind every day and night. Since he had yet to change his bed linen, he drifted to sleep breathing in her scent and filled with passionate memories of their one night together.

The thought that Natalie was downstairs had his shaft hard. He could, and he would now admit that he had it bad for her. The last seven days had been pure torture. More torturous than the agony she'd delivered that night. But in the end she had relieved his suffering in a way that could still make him tremble inside. She had delivered continuous pleasure over and over again—for someone not as experienced in the art of lovemaking like most women he'd encountered. He had surmised as much from the way her eyes lit up when they tried varied positions. He had introduced her to a lot of things in that one night and like a zealous and devoted student, she had been eager to learn.

And then there had been the way she had taken him into her mouth. What she'd lacked in skill she had made up in enthusiasm. Just thinking about what she did and how she'd done it made his shaft even more engorged and sent a rush of desire racing through his body.

Leaving his office he went into his bedroom and began stripping off his clothes deciding what he needed more than anything before coming face-to-face with Natalie was a cold shower. Otherwise, he wouldn't have any control and would be tempted to try to seduce her for another day and night of pleasure as soon as he set eyes on her.

A short while later, he stepped out of the shower and grabbed a huge velour towel to dry off. He heard the sound of her moving around right outside his bedroom door and wondered what she would think if she were to see him just as he was. He wouldn't shock her with his nakedness but would come close. With just a towel wrapped tightly around his middle, he crossed the room and flung the door open.

The woman let out a scream.

It wasn't Natalie. Collecting his wits, he ducked behind his bedroom door, cracking it open with just enough space to talk through it. She was still screaming and he knew he had to take hold of the situation by first calming the woman down. He could just imagine what she was thinking seeing a half-naked man suddenly appear.

"Would you please calm down, lady? I live here," he said with a little irritation in his voice. The woman appeared to be in her late fifties. Where the hell was Natalie?

"You're Mr. Steele?" she asked once she'd finally stopped screaming.

"Yes, I'm Mr. Steele."

"Sorry that I screamed like that but you scared me half to death. The agency said you would be at work."

Donovan knew that in all essence there was no reason for him not to be at work. He had worked at home last Friday with the clear intent of seducing Natalie. Now that he'd slept with her there was no reason for him not to have gone into the office today. But deep down he knew there was a reason. He had deliberately stayed home with the sheer purpose of seducing her again. Sleeping with her hadn't gotten her out of his system.

"I decided to work at home today. And where is my regular cleaning lady?" he asked, annoyed.

"Ms. Darwin hurt her ankle, sir."

Out of respect for the woman's age, he tried not rolling his eyes. She was old enough to be his mother.

It was bad enough she'd seen him undressed, and now she was referring to him as *sir.* Natalie was going to pay dearly for this little fiasco. "I'm aware of that," he said, trying to keep his voice calm. The woman had been frightened enough. "I'm talking about the woman who's cleaned this place for the past two weeks. I believe she's Ms. Darwin's niece."

"I don't know. I'm new. I was told to come here today. Is there a problem, sir?"

"No, there isn't a problem." *At least not with you. But I will deal with Natalie Ford. She will pay dearly for this, especially since I told her I didn't want another housekeeper.*

"Please continue your cleaning," he said, plastering a smile on his face. "I'm going to get dressed, and I'll be out of your way shortly."

"Yes, sir."

He closed the door. If Natalie thought she'd seen the last of him then she had another thought coming.

Placing a client's file aside, Natalie reached out and answered the phone on the desk. "Special Touch Housekeeping Agency."

"You've underestimated me, Natalie."

Natalie pulled in a deep breath. She recognized the deep, husky voice and knew the identity of the man on the other end of the call. And he didn't sound like a happy camper. "Is there a problem, Mr. Steele?"

He didn't say anything, but she swore she could hear his teeth gnashing. And then. "What have I told you about calling me Mr. Steele? If I remember correctly, I was Donovan last Friday night."

He'd been a number of things last Friday night, she thought. He was also the best lover she'd ever had, granted she hadn't had many to compare him with, but the one comparison she could make pushed him off the charts. "Mr. Steele, is there a reason you called?" From his tone she knew there was.

"Yes, there is a reason. I thought we understood that no one but you or your aunt would be responsible for the cleaning of my home."

Natalie smiled politely, although he couldn't see it. She had received good news earlier from Dr. Stanley and had no intention of letting him ruin her day. "As you know, my aunt is recuperating, and considering our relationship—specifically what happened between us last Friday night—there was no way I could return to your home."

"Did I force you to have sex with me, Natalie?"

His question came as a surprise. "No, of course not."

"So there's no way you can claim there was any type of sexual harassment involved, right?"

"Right, and neither am I trying to. But the key word is *involved*. We slept together, of our own free will, but we slept together nonetheless, and in doing so, we've taken our relationship from a professional one to a personal one," she tried pointing out.

"If I remember, we didn't get much sleep that night. And one has nothing to do with the other. And you were forewarned what would happen if my requests weren't followed. I enjoy my privacy and—"

"For crying out loud, Donovan," she said, annoyed enough at this point to forego professionalism. "Ms.

Harris is old enough to be your mother. She has been married for over twenty years and is not aspiring to become a cougar. She's harmless. And we did a thorough background check. The woman is trustworthy."

"Probably. But still, you defied my wishes. Meet with me at the Racetrack Café at seven tonight to discuss the situation."

Natalie frowned. "There's nothing to discuss."

"I think there is. You've made me an unhappy client. If you check the files of several of your other clients—namely Jeremy Simpkins, Harrell Kelly, Uriel Lassiter, Myles Joseph and Colin Ashford, they are clients based on my recommendations and referrals. All it would take is a phone call from me and they'll drop the Special Touch Housekeeping Agency like a hot potato."

Natalie's frown deepened, and she sat up straight in her chair. "You wouldn't do that."

"I wouldn't suggest that you try me. I'll see you tonight at seven."

Natalie slammed down the phone.

Just who does he think he is? How dare he!

She began pacing the floor. He would ruin her aunt's company just because he couldn't have things his way? So, he wanted to meet with her to discuss things. Fine. She'd meet with him, and she'd give him a piece of her mind.

Donovan drew in a long breath as he hung up the phone. Desperate times called for desperate measures, and he'd just displayed a sign of a desperate man. Of course he wouldn't do anything to hurt Natalie's aunt's business but she didn't have to know that. Besides, he couldn't think of any other way to get her to meet with him tonight. And because he didn't want her to think it was all about sex, he'd decided it would be best if they met someplace other than his home.

Now that was another mystery to be solved—that it wasn't all about sex. The intensity of their coming together had been as miraculous as it could get. Even when he hadn't wanted to think about it, when he hadn't wanted memories to invade his brain and accumulate in his mind, they had anyway.

But now he wanted to get to know the woman who had him biting at the bits. What was there about her that he found obsessive? Why had he denied himself the opportunity to bed Jean Carroll on more than one occasion because the thought of being inside any woman's body other than Natalie's, was a turnoff?

Admittedly, he was as intrigued as he was horny, and tonight he was determined to place his highly sexual state on the back burner to find out more about Natalie Ford.

Chapter 13

Still furious, Natalie walked into the Racetrack Café and glanced around. It didn't take her long to spot Donovan standing at the bar talking to another man. Her lips set in a frown, her eyes narrowed to a slit, she walked up to Donovan, got right in his face and snapped, "I'm here. Are you satisfied?"

"If he's not, I most definitely can be."

Natalie turned to the man standing with Donovan at the same time his gaze traveled over her features. She inhaled deeply. Did all Donovan's acquaintances have to look so breathtakingly handsome?

She opened her mouth to apologize for her brash manner when Donovan spoke up. "Get lost, Uri. She's spoken for. But I guess I will introduce the two of you. Natalie, this is Uriel Lassiter, a good friend of mine."

Natalie summoned a smile while extending her hand. "Sorry for being rude. Nice meeting you, Uriel."

"Apology accepted, and please call me Uri. And it's nice meeting you, as well, Natalie. Now I guess I better get lost before Donovan forgets just what close friends we are." And then after giving her one last smile, Uriel walked off.

"Come on, let's get a table," Donovan said, recapturing her thoughts while grabbing his beer off the counter.

"You may want to make it someplace private so others won't overhear what I have to say to you," she warned.

He lifted a speculative brow. "Sounds serious."

She gave him an exasperated look. "And you didn't think that it would be?"

"A man can hope. Come on, I know just the place."

She followed as he weaved through the crowd, and before she noticed just where he was leading her, he'd opened a door and ushered her inside a room that appeared to be someone's office. "This is my friend Bronson's office," he said. "He won't be here for another hour or so."

She turned on him with narrowed eyes. "I didn't mean *this* private, Donovan."

"Relax, I promise not to bite. Have a seat and get whatever is bothering you off your chest."

At that moment he looked at her chest. Except for the lone button undone at the top, her blouse was decent enough. She had dressed appropriately, not wanting to give him any ideas. But right now her nipples were hardened peaks pressing through the material of her blouse. And the man didn't miss seeing anything.

The darkening of his eyes made her pulse rate

increase. "Okay, I'll sit," she said. Anything to shift his attention from her chest.

"So what's on your mind, Natalie?"

She rolled her eyes. "You tell me since you're the one who demanded this meeting."

"Oh, yes, the issue of my replacement for a cleaning lady. I expected you to come today."

"And I told you why I didn't. We slept together so I can no longer work for you. You can stand here all day and all night and say that you employ my aunt not me, but it doesn't matter. In my mind I've slept with the boss."

"And that bothers you?"

"Yes, it bothers me." She wished he would sit down. *He* was bothering her. Standing made her totally aware of how sexy he looked.

As if he'd read her mind, he moved away from the door to lean against the edge of the desk, facing her. He slipped his hand into his pockets, and her gaze shifted first to his pockets and then to his zipper. Did the man always have to look aroused around her?

"How long have you worked for the agency?" he asked.

"Why?" She returned her gaze back to his face, certain that a blush flamed her features.

"Because you're a very beautiful woman, which accounts for the reason I'm very attracted to you," he said. "And I find it odd that none of your other male clients have ever hit on you before."

The sound of his deep and husky voice sent shivers down her spine. She inhaled deeply, thinking that now would be a good time to tell him that she did not clean

houses for a living and that she was a chemistry professor at an Ivy League university. But a part of her
couldn't risk that he would act like all the others and
feel threatened by her achievements and see her as an
intellectual geek.

"Natalie?"

"Well, believe it. All my other clients have been
nothing but gentlemen."

He chuckled. "And I'm sure none of them ever
found you in their bed. But still, I'm curious as to how
long you've been with the agency."

She shrugged. "Long enough."

"And before that what did you do?"

She wondered why he was asking these questions. "I was in school," she said, which wasn't an
all-out lie.

"Do you ever plan to go back to school?"

That question was easy enough to answer. "Yes, I
plan to go back in the fall."

He nodded. "That's good, because I'm a proponent
of education."

He didn't have to know it but so was she.

"How far along are you in your studies?"

She tilted her head back and looked at him. "Why
all the questions?"

"I'm trying to get to know you."

His response surprised her. "Why?"

Her question was a good one, Donovan thought.
Why did he want to know more about Natalie Ford?
And especially now when he needed to stay focused
on SC. They'd had another meeting in Chance's office
yesterday, and Bas had reported that suspicious ac-

tivities were still going on and that the Gleeve-Ware formula was still in high demand.

"Donovan?"

His thoughts were pulled back to Natalie. He knew it was insane, totally unreasonable to want a woman so much, but then, maybe it wasn't. That night his body had responded to her in a way it had never responded to another woman, and even now he wanted to pull her into his arms and kiss her with a passion that had his heart racing. But the wanting, the desire, had to be mutual. It had to be what she wanted too. There was only one way to find out. She had resisted his seduction once, only to come to him on her own terms. Would she do so again? It was a challenge worth probing.

"Yes?" he finally answered.

"Why do you want to get to know me?"

"Come here and find out," he said, straightening his stance and holding out his hand in an invitation.

Natalie sucked in a deep breath, disgusted with the way her body was responding to Donovan. She moistened her lips before saying in a not so convincing tone of voice, "No."

"You sure you're not as hungry to taste me the way I'm hungry to taste you? I want to taste your breasts again, put a nipple in my mouth and make love to it with my tongue. And then the icing on the cake is when I taste you there in your very feminine place. You don't know how much I want to savor that particular spot again."

The man was killing her softly with his words. She could feel herself getting drenched between the legs.

"We agreed that night was supposed to be one and done. It was just a one-night fling," she heard herself say in a breathless voice.

"Did we? Was it? And don't we have the right to change our minds if it suits our needs, our purposes and our wants?" he asked.

Should they change their minds? she wondered. And who would they hurt if they did? They were both adults who had to answer to no one. And there was no way she could deny how much she enjoyed him as a lover. So why was she fighting her desire for him? Farrah thought a full-fledged affair with him was just the thing Natalie needed, an affair that lasted as long as they wanted it to, at least until she returned to Princeton. And like Farrah had said, denying him was easier said than done.

But then there were those emotions she was trying hard to keep at bay, emotions that swamped her whenever she thought about him, or was around him, like now. She studied his features and saw the intensity in his penetrating gaze. Yes, they had the right to change their minds. She eased out of the chair and took a step toward him and placed her hand in his.

"No promises," he said, pulling her closer into his arms.

She understood and she agreed. "No promises," she repeated, realizing at that moment with a sinking heart that she was slowly drowning in emotions he was stirring within her. Emotions she'd never felt for another man since Karl. Emotions she couldn't fight any longer.

A moan flowed from her throat when he captured

her mouth with his. Immediately his taste set her entire body on fire. When he deepened the kiss with a greediness that she felt all the way to her toes, she wrapped her arms around his neck and pressed her body closer to his. The bulge behind his zipper was potent, an indication of where things could be headed, and she knew if he led her there she would hopelessly follow.

The ring of his cell phone had them pulling apart, but he didn't intend to let her go too far. He held on to her elbow while fishing the cell phone out of his jeans pocket.

"Hello." His tone was one of irritation at being interrupted.

She watched as his eyes widened and heard the concern in his voice when he asked, "When?"

And then he responded to whatever he was told by saying. "I'm on my way."

He quickly put his phone back in the pocket of his jeans and then said to her. "Come on, let's go." He had a firm grip on her hand.

She blinked. "Go where?" she asked, while letting him guide her out of the door with him.

He glanced over his shoulder. "To the hospital. One of my sisters-in-law, Jocelyn, has been rushed there."

Natalie stopped in her tracks, which caused him to do the same. Her eyes widened in alarm. "Oh, my goodness. What happened? What's wrong?"

A smile touched the corner of his lips when he said, "She's having a baby."

The rush was on, and within minutes Natalie found herself strapped into Donovan's two-seat Mercedes convertible sports car. He was racing down the interstate, most of the time not adhering to the speed limit, but she couldn't help love the feel of her hair blowing in the wind. Adrenaline was flowing through her veins. At the moment she didn't want to think about how much emission from his car was probably polluting the air. Nor did she want to consider just how the emissions were being absorbed in the upper troposphere at mid-to-high latitudes.

She glanced over at Donovan. What had he been thinking to ask her to come with him to the hospital where his family would probably be gathered? How was he going to explain her presence?

One thing she knew about being placed in unexpected situations was to be prepared whenever possible. That propelled her to say, "Tell me about your family, Donovan."

He glanced briefly at her and smiled before turning his attention back to the road. "That's a tall order since the Steele family is a big one. My grandparents had six sons and two daughters. Two sons moved from Arizona and settled here back in the sixties and started the Steele Corporation; a manufacturing company. My father was one of the brothers, and my uncle was the other. Uncle Harold died of lung cancer around twelve years ago, leaving his share of the company to his wife and three daughters, Vanessa, Taylor and Cheyenne. My father retired eight years ago and left his share to his four sons. My brother Chance is the oldest and CEO. Sebastian, whom we call Bas, is the second oldest and is a troubleshooter in the company. Morgan is brother number three and heads the research and development department, and I'm the youngest. I manage the product administration department."

She nodded. "Your cousins, the three females, do they work for the company, as well?"

"Only Vanessa. She's over our PR department. Taylor and Cheyenne have seats on the board of directors. Taylor is a wealth asset manager and she and her husband live in DC, and Cheyenne is a retired model. She and her husband live here in Charlotte and had triplets less than a year ago, so she's pretty busy these days."

Natalie chuckled. "I can imagine. Triplets. Wow. So who's having a baby now?"

"Bas's wife, Jocelyn. But in another month we'll be doing this scene again since Morgan's wife, Lena, is expecting, as well and is due to deliver in September."

He continued talking about his family, and Natalie heard the warm affection in his voice. He also told her about his other cousins that were spread all over the country and how close all Steeles were. She drew in a deep breath when he pulled into the hospital's parking lot, still not sure why he had asked her to come. But at the moment she couldn't think of any other place she'd rather be than with him.

Chapter 14

The miracle of life always amazed him, Donovan thought, gazing into the very happy and smiling face of his brother as he held his newborn baby daughter in his arms. They had named the baby Susan after Jocelyn's favorite aunt. Jocelyn's sister Leah, who'd given birth to a daughter earlier that year, had named her daughter after their mother who'd passed away when Jocelyn and Leah had been young girls.

Donovan glanced over at Natalie who was sitting in a chair next to Kylie, Vanessa and a very pregnant Lena. All four women, who'd had tears in their eyes earlier were talking to Jocelyn, who looked rather relaxed after giving birth. He looked at Chance and Morgan to find both of them staring at him instead of their newborn niece, and he knew why. They were still in shock. This was the first time he'd ever brought a woman to a family gathering of any kind, and they were curious as to why. Hell, he was trying to figure out the answer to that question himself. All he knew was that at the time he'd gotten the call from Chance to tell him that Bas was on his way to the hospital with Jocelyn, he hadn't been ready to let Natalie out of his sight.

And then he'd talked her ears off while en route to the hospital. She'd asked about his family, and that had opened him up. Instead of sticking to the basic facts, he had ended up telling her practically everything, including information about the Steele brothers' weekly Saturday morning on the basketball court. He also told her about how Chance had met Kylie, how Bas had met Jocelyn; how relentlessly Morgan had pursued Lena; how far Cameron had gone in his pursuit of Vanessa and about Cheyenne and the triplets. Never had he shared so much information about his family to any woman.

And then there were the women in his family who'd latched onto Natalie the moment he had walked into the waiting room with her by his side. He hadn't had to introduce them since they had proceeded to introduce themselves. It didn't take a rocket scientist to see they were just as shocked as his brothers.

"So what do you think about my baby girl, Donovan?"

He glanced over at Bas, who was still wearing a proud smile even after the nurse had come to take baby Susan and place her back Jocelyn's arms. "She looks tiny, not as tiny as Athena, Venus and Troy looked when they were born, of course," he said of Cheyenne's triplets who'd been born premature. "But she's still a tiny thing."

He chuckled. "It will be fun watching her grow up, and I hope when she gets older that you don't play the big bad wolf of a daddy to her dates."

Bas grinned. "I won't unless she brings home a man like her uncle Donovan."

It was a joke but Bas's words were still on Donovan's mind when he and Natalie walked out of the hospital to the parking lot. Was he really that bad that his own brother found his ways with women despicable? Bas hadn't been an angel before he'd married Jocelyn. In fact his engagement to Cassandra Tisdale gave Donovan the shudders every time he thought about it. No one knew how glad the family had been when Bas had come to his senses and broken off the engagement.

But still, Donovan knew that he would be the first to admit that none of his brothers had ever been die-hard bachelors, at least not with the concentration that he had. He was a proud playa card member. Did he have any regrets about keeping one close to his hip? Not really. But he knew that although he'd claimed otherwise, eventually one day he would settle down. He had just refused to think about doing so.

Deciding to switch gears, he thought back on his family, namely his parents. They had arrived, and thanks to his mother, there was no chance of anyone else holding the baby any time soon. And after introducing Natalie to his parents, he wanted to get her out of here before his mother could start the inquisition, which he figured would happen had they lingered.

After pulling out of the parking lot and merging with traffic, he glanced over at Natalie. She was quiet, and he couldn't help wondering what she was thinking. Like everyone else, she'd taken a turn holding the baby and he doubted he would ever forget the way she looked with the infant in her arms. She'd had that maternal look on her face, and he'd known at that moment that motherhood was definitely in her future.

"You have a nice family, Donovan."

He glanced over at her briefly. "Thanks. What about you? I know you have your aunt. Any parents or siblings?"

She shook her head. "No, I was an only child. However, I was raised by my aunt and uncle. Their son, Eric, is five years older than me. My mother gave me to my aunt and uncle when I was just a few days old and kept trucking back to California. She would visit on occasion but did nothing but cause trouble whenever she did so—usually to get money out of my aunt and uncle by threatening to take me away if they didn't pay up."

She paused for a moment, and he figured she was regrouping her thoughts, reliving the past. He couldn't help wondering if she felt deprived of her mother's love and attention.

"Her boyfriend stabbed her to death when I was ten," she said, continuing. "It had been four years since I'd seen her, and when they sent her body back here for burial she was nothing more than a stranger to me. My aunt, uncle and cousin were all the family I had and all that I needed."

"Where's your uncle?"

"He died when I was in my teens. And my cousin, Eric, is in the State Department and works for the embassy in Australia."

When the car came to a traffic light, he tilted his

head to look over at her at the same time she glanced at him. Their gazes locked, held for a second. He knew he had to ask what he should have asked her before they'd made love, but he hadn't because at the time it really hadn't mattered since it was a one-and-done sort of thing, as she liked putting it.

"Who broke your heart to make you take a hiatus from men?"

She didn't answer right away. Instead she broke eye contact with him and looked ahead through the shield. "Karl, the heartbreaker and manipulator. He practically stripped me of my self-confidence when it came to relationships by convincing me I was lacking in certain areas." She glanced over at him. "You proved him wrong."

He remained silent for a moment and then he said, "I'm glad I was able to do so."

Natalie smiled. "I'm glad, too."

The interior of the car got quiet again, and she would have loved to know what was going on inside Donovan's head. Why had he taken her to a place where he'd known his family would be congregating? Everyone had been nice but more than mildly curious. She could tell. That only led her to believe bringing a woman around his family was not his norm. She had liked everyone—his cousins, his sisters-in-law, his brothers and his parents. They'd made her feel right at home. Included. No one had asked her a lot of questions, and she was glad of that. She would not have wanted to lie to them.

She hadn't lied to Donovan just now. She'd told him about Karl. What was her rationale in doing that? It wasn't like it would mean anything to him in the scheme of things. But for some reason she had wanted him to know sharing a bed with him had been therapeutic as well as pleasurable.

"Do you mind if I drop by my house a minute to get something before I take you back to the café?"

She glanced over at him and shook her head. "No, I don't mind."

"Thanks. I appreciate it."

The clock on the car's console indicated it was a little after ten. She figured once she got back to the café she would get her car and go on to Farrah's where she would be spending the weekend. Tonight they planned to do facials and watch romantic movies until dawn if they could last that long. Usually, they would both fall asleep by midnight.

Moments later Donovan pulled into the garage attached to his condo. He closed the garage door behind them and then turned off the car's engine. He glanced over at her. "Would you like to come inside?"

She shook her head. "No, thanks. I'll just sit here until you come back."

"That might be a problem."

She stared at him a moment before lifting a brow. "And why might that be a problem?"

"I told you I needed to drop by the house to get something."

She nodded, confused. "Yes, you did say that, and what of it?"

"What I needed to drop by the house to get is *you*. So will you come inside with me, please? I want you so bad I can barely stand it."

She frowned, started to tell him that sounded like a personal problem, but when she glance down at his lap, she saw that it *was* a personal problem for him. A rather huge one.

She stared back at his face. She'd never known a man to want her this much. "Bringing me here was rather presumptuous of you," she said, her frown deepening.

"I did ask."

"No, you led me to believe you needed to get something."

"I do need to get something."

She opened her mouth to argue at his logic but then closed it, knowing it wouldn't do any good. The man gave arrogance a whole new meaning. "I'm staying put right here," she said stubbornly.

He smiled and leaned over the console, very close to her mouth and said, "Then I guess this place will have to do. At least for this."

Before she could draw her next breath, he had mingled it with his in a kiss that was so potent she felt it all the way to her toes. His tongue was dueling with hers, stroking varying degrees of desire within her. She knew the exact moment he slipped his hand underneath her skirt, expertly moving under her panties to insert his finger into the warmth of her. And then his fingers began moving to the same rhythm his tongue was using on her mouth.

Nothing about the kiss was civilized. It was as untamed and wild as it could get, and when an orgasm threatened, his mouth on hers and his fingers inside of her boldly pushed her over the edge.

"Now are you ready to go inside?" he asked a short

while later, pulling his fingers out of her while greedily licking the corners of her lips.

His words, a hoarse whisper, inflamed her body even more, and at that moment she couldn't deny him anything, especially after what he'd just given her.

"Yes," she all but whispered back. "I'm ready to go inside."

Getting out of the car, he quickly came around in front to open her door. The moment she alighted he swept her into his arms and proceeded to carry her into his home.

Not wasting any time, as soon as they passed through the back door he began stripping her naked right there in his kitchen. He then placed her on her back on his kitchen table, and then after practically tearing off his own clothes and putting on a condom, he crawled on top of her.

He gazed down at her. "This is what I wanted to come here to get. Thank you for letting me have it."

He drew in a huge breath, and in one smooth thrust he entered her, then he pulled out slightly, only to thrust into her again.

Over and over. Nonstop. Even when he felt her inner muscles clenching him and heard her soft sounds of sexual pleasure, he kept going and going. He couldn't stop. Even the pain of her fingernails digging deep into his back couldn't slow him down. And when an orgasm struck the both of them, he began giving and giving until he had nothing left to give.

At least so he thought. He began getting hard again while buried deep inside the warmth of her body.

"Natalie." He'd lifted himself up slightly to say her name and then it was on again. The only thing he could think of was that he might never get enough of her.

Natalie eased from the bed, careful not to awaken Donovan. After he had talked her into staying overnight she had called Farrah. Without going into a lot of details she cancelled their sleep-over with a promise they would do lunch next week.

She glanced over at the clock on his nightstand. It was close to five in the morning.

They had finally given the kitchen table a rest only to come upstairs to wear down his bed. Then a few hours later he had carried her back downstairs and after collecting their clothes off the floor and tidying up the kitchen, they had shared cooking duties and made omelets and coffee.

After they had eaten and were headed back up the stairs, Donovan had gotten an unexpected visitor, a man he introduced as his best friend, Bronson Scott. Just like Xavier and Uriel, Bronson was handsome as sin, and although she wasn't into auto racing, she recalled seeing his face a number of times in the newspapers as well as on the cover of *Sports Illustrated* magazine as part of a NASCAR spread. When Donovan had mentioned her car being left at the café, Bronson had offered to bring it to her and leave the keys under the mat.

After Bronson left, they had gone back to bed to make love again and had eventually drifted off to sleep. But as was the norm with her, she found herself waking up with chemical equations in her head that she needed to jot down. She didn't have her laptop, but she always kept a notepad in her purse.

Slipping Donovan's T-shirt over her head she padded in her bare feet down the stairs to get the notepad out of her purse. Then she headed back upstairs to his office. She sat down behind his huge desk and inhaled deeply, thinking that sleeping with Donovan again had not been in her plans. But the man was a master at seduction.

She glanced around the room. This was only her second time in here. The first time she had been concentrating too deeply on cleaning the room to pay close attention to the plaques on his wall and the trophies in a cabinet.

Getting up from behind the desk, she walked over to study the plaques. All but one had been presented to him for his volunteer work in the Special Olympics. The other had been presented to him for being a mentor with the Charlotte public school system.

Then there were all the basketball trophies he'd gotten while in college. She wished she could have been in the bleachers when he was running up and down the court. With his fine physique, that would definitely have been a sight to see.

Returning to the chair behind the desk, Natalie knew she had to tread very carefully where Donovan was concerned or else those emotions within her which were already teetering close to the edge, would soon lose their balance and topple over. The last man she'd thought she loved had ended up hurting her badly. She knew that, because of her mother, she didn't take rejection well, so she avoided it at all costs. Karl had taught her a lesson of what could happen if you were to let your guard down, and she could see herself falling for Donovan if she wasn't careful.

She had been working on various formulas for almost an hour when she heard a sound and glanced up. Donovan stood shirtless in the doorway wearing a pair of jeans, unzipped, and riding low on his hips. His shoulders looked powerful; the wide span of his chest was masculine, sexually compelling. His appearance was doing a number on her senses, and the degree of his sexuality set off a distinct throb in her body.

She could vividly recall everything they had done since entering his home, and the memories made sensuous shudders flow through her. And it wasn't helping matters that she was pinned by the deep intensity of his gaze.

"I woke up and you were gone. You okay?" he asked in a concerned voice.

She knew why he was asking if she was okay. Their lovemaking had been intense. She smiled. "Yes, I'm fine."

He glanced at her notepad. "What are you doing?"

She closed the notepad and pushed it aside. Now would be a good time to tell him about the chemical equations she was working on for the global warming panel, which would lead into what she did for a living. But for some reason she wasn't ready to reveal that to him now, especially when she remembered how other men had reacted, calling her a chemistry geek. She couldn't handle it if he acted the same way. But she would have to tell him soon, especially since she would be flying out on Thursday for Princeton.

"I couldn't sleep," she said, "and thought I'd come in and kill some time until you woke up."

A smile touched the curve of his lips. "I'm awake now."

He slowly crossed the room, and the closer he got the hotter the desire burned within her. "Are you sure you're fully awake?" she asked, watching his approach and thinking just how undeniably handsome he was.

"Why don't you come from behind that desk? I'll show you just how awake I am."

She couldn't help but chuckle. "Haven't you gotten enough of me already?"

"Afraid not. I have the desire to make love to you for the rest of the night. In fact I want you to spend the rest of the weekend with me."

She lifted a brow as she came from behind the desk. He scooped her up in his arms and set her down on the edge of it. "You want me to stay with you all weekend?" she asked, to make sure she'd heard him correctly.

"Yes. But that means you'll have to go to the Steele brothers basketball game tomorrow morning."

Earlier she had imagined how it would be to see him work a basketball court. "I'd love to go watch."

"It can get brutal," he warned, reaching out and sliding his hand up her legs. "Depending on how much frustration we have to work out."

She leaned in, close to his face. "Do you think you'll be frustrated?"

His hand went farther up her thigh. "Not as long as I go to bed with you tonight and wake up with you in the morning," he said huskily. "You, Natalie Ford, are the best frustration-reliever there is."

"Glad I can help, Donovan Steele."

Donovan leaned closer and captured Natalie's lips with his. Kissing her had a way of stripping his senses, making him lose control. He liked the way her tongue mingled with his, the way her taste always made him more aroused than he already was. The way he could rouse her just by touching her in a certain sexy spot, like he was doing now. She groaned deep in his mouth. He pulled back slightly, enough to break off their kiss, but then he used his tongue to trace a trail around her lips, lips he loved kissing.

He then nibbled a path close to her ear. "I need some more of you," he whispered huskily.

"Greedy," she accused in a deep moan, and he retaliated by inserting his fingers deep inside of her. Her next moan sounded deeper than the last.

"Only with you." And that was so much of the truth that it had him trembling inside. Every cell in his body was attuned to her. He never imagined being this connected to any woman.

"Then if you want me, take me," she invited.

"Gladly."

And then he went back to her mouth, fed on it greedily, while her fingers sank deep into his shoulder.

Pulling back, breaking off the kiss, he yanked his T-shirt over her head and tossed it aside, exposing her beautiful breasts. He bent his head and took a nipple in his mouth, teasing the hardened tip with his tongue.

But that wasn't enough. He wanted to be inside of her.

He drew back, looked into her face and saw her passion-glazed eyes. He then eased out of his jeans, kicked them aside and put on a condom before sweeping her into his arms and heading for the nearest wall. By the time she felt the hard surface at her back, she parted her thighs. Before she could take her next breath, he had entered her and was moving inside of her, holding her in a way that allowed him to penetrate deep.

The legs that curved around his back were tight, urgent, but not as urgent as the movement of his thrusts that were going in and out of her. When he felt her inner muscles clamp down on him, he threw his head back and actually growled.

As if the sound was what she needed to hear to push her over the edge, he heard Natalie cry out his name. She thoroughly lubricated his sex while at the same time she milked it for all it was worth.

His teeth clenched when another orgasm hit on the tail of the last, and he knew as he heard her orgasm follow his that when it came to undiluted passion, Natalie was in a class by herself.

"Aren't you the one who said you would never bring a woman to watch us play?" Bas asked his brother as they took a time-out. "What's going on? Are you and Natalie joined at the hip?"

Donovan didn't say anything as he took a huge gulp of water. After last night, they might as well be joined at the hip…as well as a number of other places. After making love in his office, he had taken her downstairs and they made love in the other rooms, as well. By the time she left tomorrow, he wanted them to have christened every room.

But to get his brother off his back, he said, "Think whatever you'd like."

He took another swig of water as he glanced up in the bleachers. Natalie sat talking to Kylie, who was there with Alden to support Chance. An uneasy feeling spiked up his spine. She looked good with his family. Like she belonged.

She had agreed to spend another night with him after checking on her aunt. But she wanted to keep their relationship a secret from the woman. Because that's what she wanted, he had agreed.

When the break was over and it was time to play another round of basketball, he glanced in the stands again. Natalie waved. He smiled and waved back.

"A gift? For me?" Natalie asked, looking at the prettily wrapped gift box Donovan had just handed to her when he joined her on the sofa.

"Yes, it's for you." A naughty grin touched his lips. "And in a way it's for me, as well."

She lifted a brow while unwrapping the gift. After the basketball game he had dropped her back off at his house when she'd felt sleepy and wanted to take a nap. That was fine since he had agreed to drop by the mall where Bronson was autographing T-shirts at a sports shop.

For some reason she wasn't surprised to open the box and find Victoria's Secret tissue paper. Then she smiled when she uncovered a very pretty sexy blue-and-white lace nightie with spaghetti straps.

"A lingerie shop was right across from where Bronson was signing," he explained. "This particular item was on a mannequin in the window, and I kept staring at it and imagining you wearing it."

He paused a second, looked up at her and then added, "I've never bought a woman something this intimate before."

Natalie didn't say anything at first. Knowing that he had done something for her that he had never done for another woman touched her deeply. And at that moment, she knew she could no longer deny the emotions she was feeling for him. She had fallen in love with Donovan.

She looked back down at the beautiful gift and knew she would cherish it always. She then glanced back at him. "Thank you, Donovan. I'll wear it tonight just for you," she said softly.

A grin touched his lips. "Just as long as you know it won't stay on you long."

She couldn't help but chuckle. "I didn't think it would."

She placed the box aside and crawled over into his lap to give him a very special kiss. Although she couldn't tell him how she felt, she wanted to show him.

Chapter 15

It was Wednesday morning, and for the first time in Donovan's life, he arrived to work late. His secretary stared as he passed her desk. He smiled. "Is anything wrong, Sandra?"

"No, sir. Are you ill?"

He couldn't help but chuckle and said over his shoulder. "No, in fact I couldn't be better."

"That's good to hear because your brother called, and he didn't sound like he was in a good mood."

Donovan stopped before opening the door to his office to ask, "And which brother is that?"

"Mr. Morgan Steele. And he wants to see you right away."

"Okay. Let him know that I'm here."

Donovan entered his office, tossed his briefcase on

the leather loveseat and immediately walked over to
the window. It was a beautiful day because the last five
days had been perfect, beginning with Friday night.

Never had he made one woman the focal point of
his weekend. And he couldn't recall, if ever, when
he'd drifted off to sleep with his body still inside of
one, connected in the most intimate way. He could
only blame it on that negligee he had bought her. She
had looked sexy in it, just like he'd known she would.
Blue was definitely her color.

He chuckled, remembering how he'd tried making
love to her in every single room in his house and, he
thought smugly, he had succeeded.

In addition to Friday, Natalie had spent Saturday
night with him, as well. She had left for a short while
on Sunday and returned on Sunday evening when they
had prepared dinner and watched a movie together,
first a chick flick and then one of his action movies.

She had left late Sunday night, and he had missed
her like crazy. Luckily he'd been kept busy at work on
Monday but had looked forward to seeing her in the
evening. He hadn't been able to talk her into staying
over on Monday, but last night she had succumbed to
his powers of seduction without much of a fight. The
results, although he'd been late for work, had been
most rewarding.

"Mr. Steele, Mr. Morgan Steele is here," his secretary interrupted his thoughts by saying over the inter-
com.

"Thanks, Sandra, please send him in."

Donovan turned from the window, and the moment

his brother walked in he could tell there was trouble.
"What's going on, Morgan?"

Morgan slumped down in the nearest chair. "There
is a spy somewhere, Donovan. Devonshire Manufacturing Company knows too much about Gleeve-Ware not
to be getting information from someplace. In Bas's
absence I'm ordering a detailed security report on
everyone who has access to the formula. This is serious."

Donovan nodded. Yes, it was serious. SC had a
major product breakthrough on their hands, and others
were trying to be the first to claim it before it reached
the market. Troubleshooting was Bas's specialty, but
he would be out of the office this week to spend time
with his wife and newborn daughter.

"You still have your copy of the report, right?"
Morgan asked, reclaiming his attention.

"Yes, but all those formulas are Greek to me."

"Well, destroy the copy you have since everything
has practically been revised, thanks to Juan. We're
keeping an updated version under lock and key, and
only the four of us and Juan will have access to it."

"No problem."

Morgan turned to leave and then paused and said,
"And just so you know, we like Natalie."

Donovan chuckled. "Thanks, Morgan. I happen to
like her, too."

"So when are you going to tell Donovan what you
really do for a living?" Farrah asked at Natalie from
across the table. The two had met for lunch, a promise
Natalie had made when she'd canceled their plans for
the weekend to spend time with Donovan instead.

Natalie shook her head, remembering this past weekend when he'd walked in on her in his office. "I'll see him later tonight, and I'll bring it up then—especially since I need to tell him I'm leaving to return home to Princeton tomorrow."

"Considering how those other guys acted once they discovered you had a working brain, do you think Donovan will have an issue with it?"

Natalie had thought about it a lot. In the beginning a part of her wasn't sure what his reaction would be, so she had kept the information to herself. But now after spending time with him and getting to know him better, she refused to believe he would feel threatened by her achievements like all the others had. "I really don't think so."

Assuming she was a housekeeper, he hadn't placed much importance on her profession before introducing her to his family. Donovan, she believed, was a man comfortable in his own skin and would have no reason to be intimidated by her career.

"Do you think he'll be upset that you haven't been completely truthful to him?" Farrah asked, taking a sip of her tea.

Natalie shrugged. "I don't know why he would be. I began feeling deep emotions for him the first time we made love. He was so different from Karl. I couldn't help but acknowledge those differences to myself, but I refused to admit I was falling in love with him."

"Why?"

"Because in my mind that was a one-night stand, so I didn't want to put my emotions out there on a lost cause. Karl, as well as those others who felt threatened by my academic achievements, made me wary."

Farrah reached across the table to take Natalie's hand in hers. "I like Donovan, and I could tell that night at the café how much he was interested in you. I truly believe things will work out between you two, although I don't know how he's going to feel knowing you'll be returning to Princeton for good in a few weeks."

"Now that's the part that scares me," Natalie said. "I'm not sure he'll be interested in a long-distance affair." She inhaled deeply. "We'll find out his thoughts on everything tonight."

The Product Trade Show couldn't get here fast enough, Donovan thought, entering his home that afternoon. He, Chance and Morgan had met with Juan Hairston for a demonstration of Gleeve-Ware, and they'd been amazed at how much progress had been made. In addition to the wear-free tires, he envisioned a number of other ways the products could enhance the lives of consumers.

It was late but Natalie had agreed to drop by. The moment he went up the stairs and stepped into his bedroom, memories of the past few days came flooding back. He still wasn't sure how it was possible to feel so happy, and a part of him was afraid he would pinch himself to find it was all a dream.

After taking a quick shower, he slipped into a pair of jeans and went into his office to get some work done before Natalie arrived. Settling into the seat behind his desk, he noticed a small notepad on the floor and recalled it was the same one he'd seen Natalie scribbling something in Friday night when he had awakened to find her missing from the bedroom and in here. He reached down and picked it up, wondering if she had a penchant to doodle like he often did.

He opened the notepad and frowned. The first page was filled with several chemical equations that looked similar to the ones Juan had been sharing with them on Gleeve-Ware for the past eight months or so. Why on earth would Natalie have a notepad filled with various formulas?

At this stage of the game, you basically can't trust anyone. Your competitor will pay top dollar for someone to steal the formula right from under your nose, using any technique they can and anyone they can.

Juan had spoken those very words to him, Chance and Morgan during their meeting today. Now those same words came down on him like a ton of bricks.

He wanted to believe that this was a coincidence, but there was a big GW on the first page above the list of equations. GW for Gleeve-Ware. And his mind was flashing one question: Why would a cleaning lady spend her time writing formulas?

He closed his eyes as several reasons came to mind— none of them he liked. That night he'd found her in this room, had she been copying the formula from the papers he had locked in his desk drawer? It would have been easy to get the key off his key ring, and he would be the first to admit she had acted rather strangely that night.

At that moment he felt as if someone had punched him in the gut. Pain of intensity he'd never felt before chilled him to the bone, and time stood still as he sat there and stared at the notepad, trying to come up with reasons she would have it. He tried like hell not to jump to conclusions.

But the more he thought about it, the more his mind was doing just that. By the time he heard the doorbell, intense anger had replaced desire.

Natalie knew something was wrong the moment Donovan opened the door, and stood back to let her enter and then all but slammed the door shut behind her.

"What's wrong, Donovan?"

"You left something behind the last time you were here," he said in a hard tone, holding up the notepad for her to see. "Out of curiosity, I thumbed through it and couldn't help noticing it was filled with formulas, something I wouldn't expect from a person claiming to be a housekeeper. Why is that, Natalie?"

She swallowed hard, wishing she had told him Friday night like she'd been tempted to do. "Because I don't do housekeeping for a living."

"Evidently." He rubbed a hand down his face and then looked back at her. "So, how much were you paid?"

Paid? "Excuse me? What are you talking about?"

"I'm talking about the fact that this notepad is filled with Gleeve-Ware formulas."

"Gleeve-Ware? I don't know what you're talking about, Donovan."

Donovan inhaled deeply, trying to quell his anger. How could she stand right in front of him and claim she didn't know what he was talking about when he had the proof right in his hand? Anger mixed with the pain of betrayal and he wanted her out of his sight now before he said or did something he would regret.

"Here," He offered the notepad back to her. "This is really useless to you since those equations are out-dated. The Steele Corporation was one step ahead of you."

She refused to take it. "Donovan, I have no idea what you're talking about, but if you just listen to me for a second, I'll be able to clear—"

"The only thing you can do right now, Natalie, is leave and don't come back. You got what you came for. Funny thing, though, it was a wasted effort on your part."

A cruel smile then touched his lips. "But not on mine. My goal was to get you back in my bed, and I succeeded in doing that."

"Donovan, I—"

"No! Please leave now, Natalie. I don't want to ever see you again."

Natalie knew that in his present state there was no way she could get through to him, so she turned and walked out the door.

"Let me get this straight. Donovan thought your notepad with those chemical equations on global warming had something to do with this project his company is working on?"

Natalie wiped the tears from her eyes. "Apparently."

She had left Donovan's house and had gone directly to Farrah's, nearly colliding with Xavier, who just happened to be leaving when she was arriving. And with Farrah still in her bathrobe and naked under-neath, it didn't take a rocket scientist to guess what the late-night visit had been about.

"He actually thinks I'm a corporate spy. Can you believe that, Farrah? Just how crazy is that? And what hurts more than anything is that he didn't give me a chance to explain. How could he so easily assume the worst about me after all the time we spent together?"

Farrah regarded her carefully. "So, what are you going to do, Nat?"

Natalie lifted her chin stubbornly. "Nothing. Eventually he'll see he made a mistake."

"And then what?"

Natalie inhaled deeply. "And then, still nothing. I refuse to love a man who can think the worst about me."

"But you already love him," Farrah pointed out.

Fresh tears appeared in Natalie's eyes. "I know, and that's why I'm hurting so bad."

Donovan paced the confines of his living room. His pain was almost unbearable, and he fully understood why.

He had fallen in love with her.

Hell. Him? The playa of all times? The man who swore no woman would ever have his heart? Yeah, well, one had definitely gotten it.

He didn't even try to figure out how and when it had happened. He was far from being a romantic, but he would guess it had been the day he had found her asleep in his bed. Something inside of him had cracked the moment she had awakened and he had gazed down into her honey-brown eyes. From that moment on, he had wanted her like he'd wanted no other woman.

And now that woman had betrayed him.

He would have to meet with his brothers in the

morning and tell them everything. He could just imagine what they'd think to discover the one woman he had brought around had been nothing more than a corporate spy.

He glanced at the clock. It was past midnight but more than likely Chance was still up. He dialed his brother's phone number.

"Hello?"

"Chance, I need you to call a meeting with everyone in the morning."

"Why? What's going on, Donovan?"

"I'd rather not say right now."

There was a pause and then Chance said, "All right, I'll arrange the meeting."

"And it would be a good idea if Juan was included."

Chapter 16

"Okay, Donovan, what's this all about?" Chance asked his younger brother when everyone had arrived for the meeting that they decided to hold in the lab. Even Bas had decided to come in, refusing to be left out of anything of importance when it came to the Steele Corporation.

Donovan stepped forward. "It's about this," he said, holding up Natalie's notepad in his hand.

Morgan lifted a brow. "What is that?"

"Something Natalie left at the house."

Chance looked confused. "Natalie?"

"Yes."

"You still haven't said what it is," Bas pointed out, no doubt trying to follow Donovan but having a hard time.

"It's a notepad filled with chemical equations."

"And your point?" Morgan asked.

Donovan was tempted to throw the notepad across the room and hit Morgan with it. "My point is that I found it very strange that she would have something like this in her possession. And with the letters GW written on every page."

Bas stared at him. "So let me get this right. Are you saying that you think your girlfriend—"

"She isn't my girlfriend. At least not anymore," Donovan snapped.

Bas rolled his eyes. "Okay, then. Are you saying that the woman you brought to the hospital last week, and the same woman you brought to our game on Saturday, could be a corporate spy?"

"Why else would she have something like this in her possession?" Donovan countered.

"Did you bother to ask her?" Chance asked.

. Donovan shrugged. "I didn't want to hear anything she had to say."

All the men in the room, including Juan, stared pitifully at Donovan for a moment before shaking their heads. Bas spoke for the group. "Donovan, you have a lot to learn about women, especially if it's a woman you care deeply about. You never accuse her of anything unless you have concrete proof."

"But this is proof," Donovan said in a frustrated voice. He could tell by his brothers' and Juan's expressions that they weren't totally convinced.

"What does she do for living?" Juan spoke up for the first time to ask.

"Her aunt injured her ankle, and she's been helping out for the past few weeks as a cleaning lady. We met when she came to clean my house," Donovan said, deciding they didn't need to know he'd found her asleep in his bed.

"And when she's not cleaning houses, what's she doing?" Chance asked.

"She said she was in school," Donovan responded, folding his arms across his chest. "And before any of you ask, I did consider the possibility that this was homework, but she claimed she was out for the summer, so she had no reason to be scribbling down chemical equations."

No one said anything for a moment and then Juan spoke up. "May I see the notepad, Donovan? It won't take me but a second to decipher the equations and tell if you're right about her."

Donovan handed it to Juan, who browsed through the pages a few minutes in silence, then looked up at Donovan. "I hope she's a forgiving woman."

Donovan swallowed. A funny feeling stirred in the pit of his stomach. "Why would you hope that?"

"Because these formulas have nothing to do with Gleeve-Ware."

"B-but the GW—"

"Stands for global warming." Juan browsed through the notepad again. "What's the name of your used-to-be girlfriend again?"

"Natalie. Natalie Ford."

A surprised glint appeared in Juan's eyes. "Natalie Ford? *The* Dr. Natalie Ford? Renowned chemistry professor at Princeton University, who just last year received a special award from the federal government for her work with NASA? And," he added, reaching across his desk to retrieve a book from a nearby bookcase, "*The New York Times* bestselling author of this book?"

Juan flipped the book to the back where a color photo of a young, but professional-looking, Natalie was on the cover. "Nice photo of your ex-girlfriend, don't you think?"

Donovan's jaw dropped, clearly stunned. "She never told me."

"Um, probably because she wasn't one-hundred percent sure about you just yet, Donovan," Chance said smartly. "Makes one wonder why."

Donovan was already headed for the door.

"If I was her, I wouldn't take you back," Morgan called after him.

"I'd never give you the time of day again," Bas added.

"I'd definitely make you suffer a little bit," Chance threw in, chuckling.

"If she does forgive you and you get back in her good graces, I'd like her to autograph my book," Juan couldn't resist saying.

Donovan didn't bother making a comment. His mind was filled with a question of significant magnitude: How was he going to win back the woman he loved?

Natalie opened her mouth to argue a point made by one of the other panelists, only to snap it closed when she saw Donovan enter the auditorium and take a seat in the back. What was he doing here in Princeton?

Refusing to let his presence unnerve her, she turned her attention back to the discussion, rebuffing her desire to look out over the crowded audience and seek him out. Their eyes had met when he entered the room, so he was fully aware that she'd seen him.

Her mind sifted through all the global warming ideology her colleagues were presenting, and she was able to rejoin the discussion and provide some opinions of her own, as well as answer several questions that were presented to her. It didn't bother her in the least that for the next hour Donovan saw just what a chemistry enthusiast she was.

After Dr. Stanley officially brought the workshop to a close and everyone began filing out of the auditorium, Dr. Lionel Walker turned in his chair and smiled at her. "Great job, Dr. Ford. You have some very interesting concepts. I would like to invite you out to dinner so we can discuss a few."

She smiled back, recognizing a hit when she heard one and inwardly wishing that she could experience with this man the same sudden electricity she'd felt with Donovan. He was young and handsome but not as handsome as Donovan.

"Thank you for the invitation, Dr. Walker, but I'll be catching a flight back to Charlotte in the morning to check on my sick aunt," she said, ignoring Donovan. Out of the corner of her eye she saw him walk up the aisle toward the stage.

"Perhaps another time? I plan to be back in Princeton in October."

She didn't want to give the man false hope. Besides, she needed to leave the stage before Donovan reached it. She wasn't ready to hear anything he had to say. His presence meant he'd discovered he had accused her falsely, but she didn't want to discuss anything with him.

Quickly easing out of her chair, she kept the smile plastered to her face when told Dr. Walker, "Perhaps. Please excuse me for running off but I have an appointment."

She rushed down the side aisle but she wasn't quick enough.

"Natalie, wait up."

She would have kept walking, but a number of people who were still hanging around had heard Donovan call her name and were glancing in their direction.

Inhaling deeply, she turned the moment he came to a stop in front of her. She plastered another smile on her face and said in a demure tone, "Donovan, what are you doing here?"

"I owe you an apology."

"Apology accepted. Now goodbye." She turned to walk off.

"Wait," he said, reaching out and touching her arm.

She turned back to him and wished he hadn't touched her. His touch sent sensuous chills through her body, making her remember how things used to be with them. "Wait for what?" she asked, trying to keep her voice calm.

"Can we go somewhere and talk?"

She chuckled lightly. "Why would you want to do that? You've apologized and I've accepted, so you can return to Charlotte now since we have nothing further to talk about."

"Natalie, I—"

"No, Donovan. Please leave. Go back to Charlotte."

"I won't go back without you. I have the company jet to take you home in the morning."

She shook her head. "No, I won't be returning to Charlotte with you. I have my own airline ticket."

He frowned. "Why are you acting this way? I thought you said you accepted my apology."

"I do, but that doesn't mean things will resume as they were between us," she pointed out. "In fact I think it's best if they didn't. It was nothing but a mistake."

"Don't say that."

"Why not when it's true?" she countered.

"Will you at least let me explain? Please."

She couldn't help but remember the tears she'd cried over him, the pain she'd endured over his rejection, his accusations. All of this could have been avoided if he had let her explain. But he hadn't, and now he wanted her to grant him the same courtesy he'd denied her Wednesday night.

"There's nothing to explain," she said, feeling her heart harden. "In fact I think it would be in both our interests not to see each other again like *you* suggested Wednesday night."

And before he could say anything to that, she quickly walked off and darted into the ladies' room.

Donovan watched her go, feeling a heavy blow to his heart. He was never supposed to fall in love. But he had. And regardless of what Natalie thought, they did need to talk. There was a lot he needed to understand, like why she hadn't been completely honest with him about what she did for a living. And he needed to explain why he had been so quick to think the worst about her. No excuse. Just the reason.

There was something different about her, something he had immediately picked up on. The Natalie he had gotten to know had never lacked fire. The Natalie he had just spoken to didn't display any emotion. His lack of trust and faith in her had hurt, and he had expected her anger. That he could deal with. But this unreceptive, unemotional Natalie was someone he could not.

If she truly expected him to walk away and leave her this way, then there was a lot she had to learn about him, about a Steele in general.

He turned to walk out of the auditorium. More than anything he was determined to bring her fire back.

Natalie glanced around her house—the first time she'd been back in almost a month. There was no use getting too comfortable since she would be leaving again in the morning. At least she didn't have any plants to worry about watering while she was away.

Princeton was a college town, bucolic yet intellectual. She had purchased the house three years ago and never regretted doing so. It was close to campus and located in a really nice neighborhood. And it was just the right size for her.

She hadn't bothered bringing more than a garment bag since she'd only planned to stay last night and tonight. She had already showered and was in her nightgown ready for bed. She had called earlier to check on her aunt, and since Aunt Earline hadn't mentioned anything about Donovan, that had her wondering how he'd known where to find her since she hadn't told him anything Wednesday night about leaving town. He hadn't given her the chance to do so. More than likely he had gotten information out of Farrah, which wouldn't be hard to believe since her best friend was convinced Donovan was the man for her. Farrah didn't know just how wrong she was.

Natalie's thoughts shifted back to that afternoon. When she'd come out of the ladies' room, Donovan was gone. She could only assume he had taken his company jet and returned home, like she'd told him. It was for the best.

She was about to head up the stairs when her doorbell rang. She felt a sudden fluttering in her stomach at the possibility it was Donovan. How would she handle it if it was? Trying to keep her cool, she crossed the room and looked out the peephole. Instead of a face, all she saw was a bunch of balloons.

"Who is it?" she called out.

"Donovan."

It *was* him. Her fingers on the doorknob began to shake. She leaned into the closed door. "What do you want?"

She wanted to kick herself for asking that question. Doing so had gotten her into trouble with him before—several times.

"Please open the door. I have a delivery for you."

She should tell him what to do with his delivery, but she wasn't that kind of person. Instead, she slowly opened the door and took a step back. He entered carrying a bunch of balloons and a bouquet of red roses.

"These are for you," he said, handing her both.

She set the flowers on the hall table and then glanced around for a place to put a dozen colorful balloons. "What are these for?"

"No special reason," he said, glancing around. "I had a hard time getting them. It seems most businesses in this town close at dinnertime."

After placing the balloons down she folded her arms over her chest. "What are you doing here, Donovan?"

He inserted his hands into the pockets of his slacks. She thought that he looked good, as usual. "You said you accepted my apology, but you didn't say it with passion."

"Excuse me?"

"Passion, Natalie. That's the one common denominator we've had from the beginning. I have a feeling it's slipping away."

She had news for him: it was already gone. She lifted her chin. "I don't want to talk about it."

"That's good because I don't want to talk about it, either," he said, walking into her living room. He dropped down on her sofa and began to remove his shoes and socks.

"What do you think you're doing?"

He glanced up at her. "Bringing the passion back."

His lips curved into a smile, the kind that always gave her goose bumps. Made her wet. It was the smile that made her want to do naughty things with him. She stiffened at the thought. "I'm going to have to ask you to leave, Donovan."

"You can ask, Natalie, but that doesn't mean I'll do it. In fact, I can guarantee you that I won't."

That spiked her anger. "You think you can just stay here, against my wishes?"

"Pretty much, mainly because the rift between us is just as much your fault as it is mine. I admit that I should not have jumped to conclusions," he said, standing up and pulling the shirt out of his pants. "But you aren't completely blameless. Had you told me the truth from the beginning, that you were a chemistry professor, I would not have had a reason to think you were a corporate spy. Granted, I was swift to make a judgment and I apologize for that, but there's a reason why I did it."

She tried not to notice he was now unbuttoning his shirt. "Is there?"

"Yes. I felt myself falling for you. You were too good to be true, and deep down, a tiny part of me wanted to believe you really weren't true. So when I found what I thought was proof that you weren't the woman I thought you were, I jumped on it. I apologized for it and you said you accepted my apology. Yet, you're acting cold, unemotional and dispassionate toward me. I want the old Natalie back."

"You can't have the old Natalie back."

He stood in the middle of her living room, shoeless and shirtless. "Do you care to bet on that?"

No, she didn't care to bet on it, not when he was looking at her like she was a piece of chocolate he planned to gobble up. She took a step back. He actually assumed—even after everything—that he could actually just walk in here and expect things to be as they were before.

"I don't think that," he said as if he'd read her mind. "There are a number of things we do need to straighten out—like why you didn't tell me everything in the beginning. We will get to that. But first, we need to get to this."

His hand went to the zipper of his slacks. She saw the huge bulge there and remembered the last time she'd seen him in such a state and how she had taken matters into her own hands. Literally. But she didn't want to think about that. She didn't want to remember.

But when he began easing down his zipper, memories flooded her—every tantalizing detail—and her mind became jammed with all kinds of thoughts, jumbled with all sorts of memories.

"Will you come over here or do I have to come over there?"

She knew what she wanted to say but she couldn't form the words. He took her silence as indecisiveness and said, "Before either of us takes a step, I think you ought to know something, Dr. Natalie Ford."

She swallowed. "What?"

"I love you very much. I didn't think I would or could say those words to a woman, but I'm saying them to you."

He loved her? Actually loved her? Before she could let her heart fill up with joy, she had to know one thing. "And what about what I do for a living?"

"What about it? Should it matter?"

She shrugged. "It did to other men. They considered me a chemistry geek."

Donovan held steadfast to her gaze. Now he understood, at least he thought he did. But to make sure, he asked, "Did other men find what you do for a living a turnoff or something?"

She nodded. "Yes."

"It's their loss for not getting to know the real you. The passionate you. I don't care about you being a chemistry geek because in my bed you are a sexual goddess. You make me feel things no other woman has ever made me feel."

He took a step forward. "You're mine, Natalie. You became mine the first day I saw you in my bed. I later made you mine in that same bed. The first for me and any woman. And you've technically christened my entire house. There's not a single room I can go in without thinking of you, without remembering making love to you in it."

He glanced around. "And now I want to do the same for yours. I want to leave my mark in every room in this house, so whenever you're here without me, you *will* remember."

"That's an ambitious goal, don't you think?"

He chuckled. "Yes, but one I plan to achieve, starting now. In here."

She stood there, watching as he removed his pants, his briefs and then sheathed himself in a condom. Her mind barely registered what he was doing. Instead it was still fixed on the words he had spoken earlier. *I love you very much.* How could he possibly mean it? She knew how she felt about him, but how could he love her back?

"Natalie." She blinked and then realized he was there, standing right in front of her. He had come to her. Naked. For several long moments his eyes studied her, and she felt the intensity of his gaze throughout her body.

"Now for your clothes. Strip for me," he suggested in a soft, taunting tone.

She wouldn't know where to start. But for him, she knew it would come naturally. She took a step back and eased her bathrobe off her shoulders, letting it fall in a pool at her feet. Her gown wasn't anything sexy, definitely nothing like the lingerie he'd purchased for her last week. Instead she wore white-cotton baby-doll pj's. But from the way he was looking at her, she could have worn another Victoria's Secret creation.

"You're slowing down, Natalie."

She blinked, realizing she had.

"I'm not sure how long I can hold out and behave myself," he said.

Her gaze traveled past his chest down to his middle and saw what he meant. Amazing. She smiled. Her pj's might be simple, but he was making her feel sexier by the minute. It didn't take her any time after that to remove her sleepwear. Then she stood there, facing him and just as naked as he was.

He didn't say anything, but she knew what he was thinking. He took another step forward, and her heart began beating fast. Then faster. And then he was there, right in front of her, wrapping his arms around her, sliding his palms all over her back, cupping her bottom and then returning his hands to the center of her back. And before she could blink, utter a single word, he had her off her feet and into his arms.

He stared down at her. "There's one thing you need to know about me. About any Steele."

"What is that?"

"We love forever," he said.

And then he lowered his mouth to hers, kissed her in a way that only he could, giving her all of his love, his emotions, his heart.

She kissed him back, tasting his urgency. She

murmured a soft moan when he placed her on the sofa, breaking off their kiss.

He dropped to his knees and gazed down at her. "I will cherish you and your body for as long as I live, Natalie. That is my promise to you. I will love you, be there for you and I will always be proud of what you do. Admire your work. Honor you. And belong to you. Only to you." Then he leaned closer to reclaim her mouth, as he continued to stroke the flames of desire. Doing what he'd said he would do, restirring her emotions.

Donovan kissed her with all his heart. If he was doing so with the fervor of a starving man, it couldn't be helped. He was starving for her, to savor her, taste her, claim her irrevocably as his. After tonight there wouldn't be any questions, no lingering doubts about what they meant to each other. They still had some talking to do, reassurances to make, but right now, at this moment, more than anything he wanted to restore her passion, passion he had foolishly taken from her.

He broke off the kiss and settled his mouth near the curve of her neck and placed a passion mark there, officially claiming her as his. And then his mouth moved lower to her breasts. The moment he latched on to a nipple, her lips parted and she released a soft moan.

Hungry for her in a way that he had never been hungry for another woman, he sucked her nipples shamelessly and with a desperation he felt in his engorged sex. She began shifting restlessly about as passion began to build. Then his hands, which had brought her to climax so many times he'd lost count, stroked her feminine core. She was wet. She was hot. She was ready.

With the force of a magnet, his mouth was pulled

lower, down to the center of her legs where he buried his tongue, replacing his fingers deep inside of her. She nearly came off the sofa but he held tight to her hips, refusing to let her go anywhere.

He heard her say his name over and over again, coherently and incoherently. It didn't matter. What mattered was the fact that she was no longer emotionless with him. He had rebuilt her fire, her passion, with one hell of an intimate seduction.

And when her body seemed primed for an orgasm, he pulled away and joined her on the sofa, positioned his body in place over hers. He glanced down and whispered softly, "I love you, Natalie."

And then he eased his body into her, penetrated her hot, wet folds, lifting her hips with his hands to assure a snug fit.

He threw his head back. Being inside her felt good. It felt right. This was where he belonged. And then he began moving, thrusting in and out of her, losing himself in her passion.

The more he stroked, the more she squeezed him, clenched him with her inner muscles, pulled everything out of him.

"Donovan!"

"Natalie!"

They climaxed together. Simultaneously. And with an intensity that took his breath away. The orgasm shook him to the core, as waves of pleasure washed over them. And he knew inside of her would forever be his home.

"Will you marry me?"

Natalie opened her eyes and looked up to see Donovan gazing down at her. They had moved from the living room and were now on her stairway. Their bodies were still connected and not surprisingly, he was still hard inside of her. He had an intense sexual hunger, and she enjoyed feeding it.

She wrapped her arms around him tight. "Only if we can have a long engagement."

He lifted a brow. "How long?"

"Um, at least until June. I need to wrap up the school year here before I can move to Charlotte."

"You don't have to. I can move here and telecommute. That shouldn't be hard to arrange."

She appreciated him considering doing such a thing but he didn't have to. "No, I want to move back to be close to Aunt Earline. With Eric out of the country, it's for the best and besides, it's time I come out of the classroom and do other things. I like babies."

He smiled, thinking about his newborn niece. "I like babies, too."

She shifted to sit up, and he couldn't do anything but ease himself out of her. For now. She looked over at him. "Tell me why you thought I had betrayed you, Donovan."

As best as he could, he told her about Gleeve-Ware and, not surprisingly, with her chemical background, she understood and gave Juan high praises for his achievement. "That product will revolutionize the rubber and plastics industry," she told him. "That's wonderful. I can't wait to see everyone's reaction come November."

They talked some more, and she shared with him why she had been reluctant to tell him that she was a college professor, about how in the past men had always felt threatened by her achievements.

"Where they felt jealousy toward your work, Natalie, I can only feel admiration."

"Oh, Donovan."

She fell into his arms and he held her tight. She twisted her head a little and met his lips. Pleasure tore through her the moment he inserted his tongue in her mouth.

Moments later, he pulled back. "Time to make it to the bedroom, sweetheart."

She chuckled. Just as well. They had made love in the kitchen, dining room and bathroom downstairs. "Which one? I have three."

He chuckled as he stood with her in his arms. "Tonight we will hit all three."

And she had no reason not to believe him. She had a man who was forged of steel.

* * * * *

Coming in November 2009,
read Uriel Lassiter's story in Brenda Jackson's
new six-book series—
BACHELORS IN DEMAND.
Also, coming in 2010,
meet the STEELES OF PHOENIX!

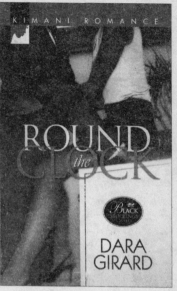

REQUEST YOUR FREE BOOKS!

2 FREE NOVELS
PLUS 2 FREE GIFTS!

KIMANI™ ROMANCE

Love's ultimate destination!

KROM09

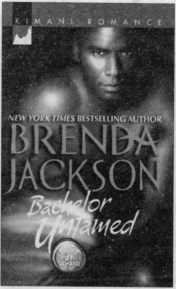

8/09

ARABESQUE®

CELEBRATE ARABESQUE'S 15TH ANNIVERSARY!

2009 marks Arabesque's 15th anniversary!

Help us celebrate by telling us about your most special memories and moments with Arabesque books. Entries will be judged by the Arabesque Anniversary Committee based on which are the most touching and well written. Fifteen lucky winners will receive as a prize a full-grain leather duffel bag with the Arabesque anniversary logo.

How to Enter: To enter, hand-print (or type) on an 8 ½" x 11" plain piece of paper your full name, mailing address, telephone number and a description of your most special memories and moments with Arabesque books (in two hundred [200] words or less) and send it to "Arabesque 15th Anniversary Contest 20901"—in the U.S.: Kimani Press, 233 Broadway, Suite 1001, New York, NY 10279, or in Canada: 225 Duncan Mill Road, Don Mills, ON M3B 3K9. No other method of entry will be accepted. The contest begins on July 1, 2009, and ends on December 31, 2009. Entries must be postmarked by December 31, 2009, and received by January 8, 2010. A copy of these Official Rules is available online at www.myspace.com/kimanipress, or to obtain a copy of these Official Rules (prior to November 30, 2009), send a self-addressed, stamped envelope (postage not required from residents of VT) to "Arabesque 15th Anniversary Contest 20901 Rules," 225 Duncan Mill Road, Don Mills, ON M3B 3K9. Limit one (1) entry per person. If more than one (1) entry is received from the same person, only the first eligible entry submitted will be considered. By entering the contest, entrants agree to be bound by these Official Rules and the decisions of Harlequin Enterprises Limited (the "Sponsor"), which are final and binding.

NO PURCHASE NECESSARY. Open to legal residents of U.S. and Canada (except Quebec) who have reached the age of majority at time of entry. Void where prohibited by law. Approximate retail value of each prize: $131.00 (USD).

VISIT **WWW.MYSPACE.COM/KIMANIPRESS**
FOR THE COMPLETE OFFICIAL RULES